1.

The moonlight shone through the dark gray clouds in the sky, only a tiny small star peeked out here and there. There was a brief gust of wind that stirred the waves on the water of the old Wishing Fountain at the stud farm of the old master Demetrisio. The fountain, as many people sometimes say, has always been here. It was built by an ancient ancestor of Demetrisius about three hundred years ago, and this ornamental edifice has never been moved from there, nor has the water been taken out. It had a number of ornamental fish that lived there, as well as a group of loud frogs that always worked devotedly at night for the purpose of their symphonic frog orchestra with loud and persistent croaking.

On the surface of the water in the "Fountain of Wishes" there were beautiful water lily leaves and flowers, and next to the fountain stood a monument to one of the best racehorses of the boss Demetrisio – the horse Wicky.

Now it was night. Across the grassy area, as if afraid of someone, a yellow domestic cat Fasel ran over. He looked left and right in dismay, as if he feared that he might be discovered in his newfound midnight action. Firmly in his mouth, as if he feared that it might fall out, he was holding an old gold coin which he had so honestly stolen from the table of Master Demetrisio. Of course, you're wondering what a yellow, country cat needs a gold coin, and that's in the middle of the night while he rushes to the fountain in amazement.

Namely, it was said that in the depths of the Old Fountain there was an old Blue Spirit who made wishes come true; All that was needed was for someone to throw a gold coin into the water on the night of the full moon. When the gold coin fell to the ground of these vague depths, the old Blue Spirit would awaken from its perennial slumber, rise to the surface of the water, and make all sorts of wishes come true to anyone who wished for something nice.

So the yellow-orange cat Fasel now somewhat proudly, but perfectly happy to have managed to get hold of the fountain with that gold coin, stood on the edge of the edge and stared for a moment at his vague reflection in the water and the moonlight that was like a lantern now above his head.

He closed his eyes for a moment, opened them and then decided that now was the ideal time to realize his intentions. He dropped the gold coin into the water, which fell and fell, until at last it landed on the ground where there were already a few old, somewhat blackened gold coins, which were now here as monuments that once upon a time, a very long time ago, someone woke up the old Blue Spirit from these depths.

And as soon as the gold coin touched the ground, blue smoke arose like clouds, from where the figure of the old Blue Ghost quickly moved towards the water. As he swam towards the surface of the water, the eternal sleeper – the Blue Ghost – yawned several times, as if wondering what kind of human soul was waking him up again after almost a hundred and thirty years of peaceful and beautiful eternal sleep.

As soon as he came to the surface, where he had already been several times, and where he had not been touched by the sight of that courtyard, which had certainly changed several times in the past period, but the old Blue Ghost never paid attention to the changes, he looked around. But now he did not see any man or woman, or maybe even a child. He looked around for a while, somewhat intrigued by the fact that someone had thrown in a gold coin and then apparently sneaked in for no reason.

It was only then that he was surprised when he saw a yellow-orange cat sitting at the edge of the fountain and watching him calmly, somewhat frightened by the fact that he had managed to awaken his spirit.

"So," said the old Blue Ghost, staring at the cat, who seemed to be breathing a little deeply, "what do we have here?" You are, therefore.

- I'm a cat.

- So we have a cat from this old Demetrisio estate, right? - the old Blue Ghost put his hands on his hips, having previously set up his black top hat.

- Yes, my name is Fasel.

- Beans? What a strange name for a cat. So, the cat woke me up from my peaceful beautiful sleep? Surely you have a special wish? – the ghost stared at him. For a moment, he put on his black hat, which he always wore and of which he was proud. – And so far, I have never made any special wishes come true for some cats.

- You always have to have a first time – nodded Fasel the cat, hoping that this ghost would make his wish come true as soon as possible, so that no one would see him calmly and nicely discussing with that old ghost on this fountain. No one could see him now.

- Then, what special and spectacular wish does a cat have? – raised the eyebrows of the Old Ghost, who had already heard various wishes from various people, so almost nothing could surprise him anymore.

- I'd like to become a merman.

- Merman?

Yes, the mermaid. I'd like to have a long nice tail and yes ...

Although he wanted to explain everything nicely, Fasel the cat didn't have time for that. As he did not like to dwell on that surface for a long time, the old Blue Ghost lifted him in one fell swoop from the edge of the fountain where Fasel was sitting, and created a somewhat golden-orange smoke around him, where Fasel the cat found himself above the water in one fell swoop, his hair disappeared, and first a golden-copper glittering tail was formed, and it stretched out like a slingshot and changed into the figure of a beautiful merman. For a few moments the old Blue Spirit held him above the water, and then suddenly the now marble Fasel slammed into the water. It lingered on the surface for a few seconds, and then, finally aware that it had become a marman, it disappeared into the depths of the old Fountain of Desire. At the same time, the figure of the old Blue Ghost disappeared, and he returned to the bottom of the fountain again calmly and peacefully to devote himself to his peaceful sleep, in the fervent desire that he would not be awakened again for the next few decades, because it was tiring for him to get up every hundred years.

Of course, Merman Fasel was delighted to finally find himself in this double underwater world that he could only dream of until a moment ago. He saw many small fish swimming, frogs jumping here and there stealthily behind huge leaves of algae, but as soon as they saw him, and he was completely unknown to them, they hid.

He realized that the underwater world beneath the fountain was not small at all, that it was a large underwater lake full of animal and plant life, which, Merman Faschel thought, would be much better seen the next day when there was sun and light.

And of course, that this wonderful idyllic harmoniously conceived life of a merman with a golden tail, was short-lived. The very next day, a big and unavoidable problem arose for the beautiful Merman life.

And this is how it went.

Namely, at the Demetrisio Stud Farm, in addition to the owner Demetrisio, the best riding horses in the country, workers and occasional seasonal riders, during the summer there lived a beautiful Demetrisio's daughter named Desdemona, whom everyone always called by a short name – Dessy. I've forgotten what her real name was.

Dessy was a beautiful and slender eighteen-year-old girl who was always in boarding school during the year, and in the summer she would spend her days at her father's stud farm. She was very educated, spoke two or three languages, knew the etiquette rules perfectly well, and often wore pink skirts and dresses with black puff boots and red knee-high boots. She also spent a lot of time playing the piano, writing poems in her scrapbook, or writing beautiful love letters to her fiancé, Gianna, who lived in Rome, fantasizing about some impossible romantic love that she knew she certainly had no chance of experiencing during the summer, especially not at her father's stud farm . Falling in love with a horse or a foal seemed impossible .

In those days, she had a task assigned to her by her father. Namely, the statute of the monument to the horse Wicky should have been coated with white varnish. This was Dessy's task that she had been doing quietly for two days, and that morning she decided to finally bring it to an end.

With a bucket of white paint in her hands and a suitcase with all sorts of brushes for spreading, this beautiful young girl came out of the workshop and calmly headed towards the old "Fountain of Wishes". She hummed a song she had learned that month and stared at the statue of Wicky for a few moments, remembering all the trophies that horse had won at the horse races at the city's Hippodrome and how much money and fame it had brought to the Demetrisio Stud Farm itself. Everyone said that there would soon be no great riding horse again, for which many said that he obviously had some unusual powers that he had acquired by the circumstances of an unusual disappearance for up to three days.

Now it was expected to finish the process of painting the back of that statue. And for a moment she stared at the surface of the water, where among the leaves and flowers of the water lily she saw something that had completely drawn her attention with its sparkler. For a moment, she hid behind a statue of Wicky the horse , staring at the large golden tail that appeared below the surface of the water.

'- Is there a big goldfish here? – she asked herself with enthusiasm and sincere interest. – Or is it some big new species of snake?

And completely determined to find out what kind of creature had protruded its golden tail to the surface of the water, Dessy hid behind this large statue that stretched in all its height of three or four meters. For a moment, the golden tail would appear, and then it would disappear from her view again.

Merman Fasel, of course, did not even think about the fact that it was not entirely appropriate to play on the surface of the water in the morning and slingshot his tail delighted with his acquired water harmony, so now he swam close to the surface of the water, aware that the best thing in this world that any cat could wish for was to become a merman in that fountain.

Dessy was completely intrigued by the swimming of this unusual creature in the water, and then what happened to many sailors who met beautiful mermaids in ancient times happened – she saw a merman in her fountain for the first time. And of course, she fell in love at first sight.

Namely, delighted with its water harmony, the Merman Fasel finally peeked above the surface of the water. She put her hand to her mouth to hide the exclamation of delight when she saw his dark beautiful hair and wide beautiful shoulders. She stared at his figure as if enchanted, fully aware that the best thing a young girl could have in her father's fountain today was certainly a marman. For a while, he swam casually, splashing his golden tail on the surface of the water, completely amused by the fact that it was nicer to swim in the water like a marman, than like an ordinary domestic fat cat. Meanwhile, Dessy, who had seen the merman for the first time now, walked slowly towards him.

He didn't notice her until Dessy grabbed him with her hands and quickly pressed a quick and powerful kiss on his right cheek, leaving a trace of her lipstick.

Finally aware that Dessy had noticed him and that he was obviously completely careless, Merman Fasel stared at Dessy, whom, of course, he knew very well as a cat, and whom he considered arrogant and conceited, like Daddy's daughters, and also only children. Now Bro felt the cheek where she had kissed him, aware that as a cat he had never received a kiss from her, except a little patting on the head or occasionally pulling his tail. Now he was looking at her looking at him with eyes of sincere adoration, that he realized that it would be best for him to retire to the depths of the underwater lake as soon as possible, I'm sure you'll get something else from Demetrius, and it's not going to be a nice kiss.

So he swam quickly under the surface of the water, aware that Dessy, like Wicky the horse, remained there a little stiffly standing and watching the water, eager to see him again.

- I don't think this will be good for me at all - concluded Merman Fasel reluctantly, "if she decides to watch what I'm doing all the time. Nothing of my beautiful water idyll, nothing of splashing on the surface of the water, nothing of anything! – he said a little angrily, aware that if she fell in love with him now, it would be a big problem in his new life that he was counting on. But now he didn't have any new gold coins to awaken the old Blue Ghost again and ask him to take Dessy to some such wonderful places as Paris or Rome, for the long haul, and in one direction.

CHAPTER TWO

The statue of Wicky the horse was covered with a large white tarpaulin that morning. And in front of him there were a lot of journalists and people. It was a gathering that boss Demetrisio had been counting on – everyone wanted to take a picture next to the statue of his best horse Wicky again and broadcast the press conference where he talked about what it was like to be the best riding horse breeder in the country.

In addition to his love of horses, the fact that he was engaged in the stud farm and the work of which there was an abundance for three or four days a week, on other working days the owner Demetrisio was also engaged in his other activities. He had two banks that were among the top 10 banks in the country, an oil refinery, and he was involved in the business of a shipyard.

He lost his wife in a car accident a long time ago, and he took care of his daughter through a governess or sent her to a wealthy boarding school in Switzerland. Thus , he was completely free and free from serious paternal obligations for most of the year, and Dessy was an exemplary and obedient daughter with whom he never had big problems.

For a few moments, the now boss, Demetrisio, was approaching with his worker, Salikil, towards the excited small crowd of journalists and some observers. He stared proudly at the statute of the horse, which had been so devotedly arranged by his daughter the other day, that he wondered why Dessy was suddenly spending so much time at that old ordinary fountain, when she had never congratulated or paid attention to her before.

- Do you see Salikil, finally the statue of the best horse will be arranged in the yard! – said the boss Demetrisio , who seemed to be waiting to finally remove the tarpaulin from the statue and show it in new whiteness.

- Yes, yes - nodded the worker Salikil who seemed to have always worked at that stud farm, and always seemed a bit stupid - Wicky's horse is your best horse! - he said what was absolutely true.

Boss Demetriso remembered some memorable great races at the Hippodrome.

He's won a lot of trophies.

-Yes, yes! He's had very, many successful races.

- I think more than 20! - said the boss Demetrisio, aware that he had never congratulated or counted how many gold trophies this unusual horse had won.

In a few moments, the workers saw what everyone had been waiting for with sincere enthusiasm – they removed the tarpaulin from the statue, so now Wicky was highlighted and freshly painted. There was still a trace of white paint on the grass in some places, Dessy as if she had dabbled a little too much paint around on the last day...

- Beautiful statue! – said one of the workers, aware that the statue had been here a week ago, but not as beautiful as it is now.

- He represents the most famous horse from the Hippodrome, certainly at his best - said another worker who held one end of the white tarpaulin.

The workers then took shelter a little further away, and the boss Demetrisio, accompanied by the worker Saliquilo, moved forward. He stood in an upright position so that journalists and photojournalists could take pictures of him.

This is going to be the most fun part of this place!

Salikil, who had never liked crowds, nor to be in the center of attention as he did now (although he was not the center of attention, but a horse), now felt mostly uncomfortable, but he did not show it quite clearly. For a moment he watched the intrigued journalists staring at the statue, aware that it was best for him that he was just an ordinary worker. That it could never be, let's say – a monument or something like that.

- I agree with that! - the boss replied quietly to Demtrisio.

- And me! – confirmed the other worker.

- Boss Demetrisio, I think you should now invite the media of the whole country - suggested the worker Salikil. It was a very clever suggestion.

Demetrisio thought for a moment.

-Media? Journalists?

- I agree with that - said the other worker, as if he wanted to give the whole idea a real tailwind.

Why should I call them? – asked the boss Demetrisio. Although he loved the bank, power and money, he never liked to show all that luxury in front of the public.

- Well, since the horse Wicky is now the most famous racehorse in the city, the champion at the Hippodrome, you need to convey to the public that he now has his own statue - explained the young worker Salikil.

- And right with you! I'm here on this property...

Demetrisio also saw the benefits of all this. News of the statute of the best horse would contribute to the price of his other riding horses. He would sell them much more expensive.

-Yes. I think I should do that in the future...

- It will be a sensation, I'm convinced ... – said the other worker. The tarpaulin was put aside, the smaller number of journalists and reporters watched the sensual display of the expensive statue...

And so the owner Demetrisio ordered a large conference to be organized for his best and most expensive horse. Wicky was the best riding horse at the Hippodrome, winning many beautiful gold goblets that were now on the shelves in the boss Demetrisio's office.

And whether this was a truly ordinary day for the estate, the only unusual fact in all of this was that there was no beautiful, young Desdemona anywhere.

In a beautiful room on the third floor was Dessy's room. A huge room with a large, crystal chandelier, overlooked the courtyard and the old fountain. Although Dessy once complained about not getting a room in the front of the house, now this fact seemed fantastic to her. There's nothing better than a magical view of the fountain.

In addition to the huge crystal chandelier, there was also a large mirror on the wall with a gold frame that was more characteristic of Wheeler's tapestries. There was a large wardrobe with many dresses and clothes that she had never worn, or had worn maybe once, a closet with mostly red shoes and boots of various shapes and models, a closet where she kept her jewelry and a rack in front of which she looked at herself. And so she is now, humming merrily, completely unaware that she seems to be in love from a mile away, she stood in front of that mirror and brushed her light brown hair. True to her eternal appearance, she just put a headscarf on her head and then quickly smeared her mouth with red lipstick, aware of her beauty and reflection in the mirror. She put on her new red boots, and then she heard a loud knock on the door.

She looked towards the door, not even knowing who she should expect.

- Forward!

He calmed down into the room and slowly, squirming a little as if she had a stone in her shoe, the maid Merkez walked in. An elderly maid who had been working on the property for several years now calmly looked at the young girl who had just stood in front of the mirror again.

-I've brought you a letter! - said Merkez, a maid, who, as was customary at the stud farm, was holding the letter on a silver ribbon.

Dessy, for a moment, was confused and surprised. She stared at the tray, even though she didn't care about the old fountain at all.

- Letter? What kind of letter?

The maid Merkez patiently said to her:

- Your fiancé... From Rome ...

It was as if it had only occurred to Dessy that morning that, well, who would have thought, she had a rich and clever fiancé in Rome, she just calmly ran her hand over her forehead.

- Ah, Gianni!

Suddenly, she nodded as if she didn't care. She looked at herself in the mirror again, as if she wasn't happy with something. She quickly took off her hairband and put on a hairband. Like that. That's better," she concluded quickly, pleased with the reflection she saw.

The maid Merkez was completely surprised by her obvious nonchalance and utter disinterestedness.

- He writes to you!

Merkez the maid handed her the tray with the letter, but Dessy did not take it in her hands, much to her surprise. She just kept running her hand through her hair and acting as if it was something that didn't concern her in the slightest.

- He is really very bored. Isn't it, Merkez?

The maid, Merquez, who didn't even know why she felt a little stupid in those moments, just stared at the tray with the letter, wondering how she might feel if she were in Dessy's place and had such a handsome, handsome fiancé as Gianni.

- Why do you think so? - asked the maid Merkez.

-Well... he writes me letters all the time...

- That's nice of him - concluded the maid Merkez, noting that Gianni was really romantic. These were beautiful qualities that were worth cherishing.

Dessy finally decided to turn to her. She put her hands on her hips, tapping her foot on the floor as if she were losing some of her innate and handsome patience.

Heartbreaking lyrics, lyrics of songs...

The maid, Merkez, nodded her head.

I'm glad he's so romantic. Don't you think so?

-Well, no! - replied Dessy, who turned slowly towards her and shrugged. Now she didn't feel like talking about Gianni and his poems and letters at all. - It would be very useful and nice if I was also in love with Gianni.

The maid widened her eyes as if in surprise. It was as if she expected to hear everything, except for the sentence that she fervently hoped the young girl would never say in front of her father.

- Aren't you?

Dessy, who was hurrying out towards the fountain, towards the water into which she had so much wanted to immerse herself, now saw that it would be necessary for her to tone down her newfound tendency to worship the old fountain a little. Someone might find out that there was a beautiful merman living in her whose name she didn't even know, and then what could happen? She couldn't even think about the consequences of all this.

- Well, no!

The maid, however, couldn't help but be surprised by her apparent lack of interest. Every other girl would rush to the tray, tearing off the cover of the letter to see the kind words, kind texts, outpourings of love ... Dessy looked as if she had received a bill to collect debts or a letter that had something like anthrax in it.

- But why are you marrying him, then? - asked the maid Merkez.

- I'm not getting married! At least not yet! And I hope I won't. It was all because my dad insisted that we get engaged. Dad didn't even ask me if I loved Gianni ... – Dessy explained to her, although she didn't feel like talking about Gianna and the engagement now. She didn't even feel like talking about her father, whom Dessy sometimes thought really had no ear for falling in love or for love. Surely all bankers are like that – she consoled herself – they only love money.

- But I think he loves you!

- Possible. But the letters are not proof of this. Anyone with the slightest bit of wisdom can write 5 heartbreaking romantic sentences, but that doesn't mean they feel love. Or anything like that," Dessy explained, seeing that it might be a good idea for her to write a few kind words to Gianni and thank her for the heartbreaking letters he'd sent her. That way, if she just keeps silent, and stands in front of that fountain, maybe she could become truly suspicious to someone.

Merkez, the maid, who no longer felt like standing in the middle of that room with that tray, now calmly put the letter away. She continued to stare at her in disbelief.

- So you won't read the letter?

Dessy looked at the envelope with a look that might have looked at a pile of dead fish or as a breeding ground for dangerous poisonous snakes. She just shrugged her shoulders calmly, eager to wait for the old maid to go with some of her business and stop telling her about Gianna. If it hadn't been for the letter, Dessy wouldn't have remembered that Gianni existed. And what kind of love is it anyway – when it is necessary for the maid Merkez to remind her of all this?

- Well, I'll read it once. I'm sure I will! But not now! And not today! She calmly walked over to the large open window and quickly looked outside. - Maybe not this week, not this month ... Hey Merkez, it's going to be a mess out there now! I see a lot of workers... Ahhhh What's going on out there now?

Merkez the maid looked at the window, but now she didn't feel like looking at the hectic and noisy crowd of all kinds of journalists and photojournalists.

-Well, I think they finally presented a statue of Wicky the horse next to that old fountain this morning, - she replied calmly.

Dessy looked a little anxiously at the water in the fountain. What if someone saw it? What if her beautiful marman splashed its beautiful golden tail a little on the surface of the water? What would happen then? The horror of the crowd of photographers flashing around, taking pictures of him, then catching him, taking him away, and she would never see him again. Okay, she'd seen him once, but that seemed enough for a lifetime. That had been her wonderful little sweet secret, and now that secret was in danger of being seriously threatened. She bit her lower lip a little scared. It was as if everything had been conspiring against her and her dear desire to be next to her merman.

I've seen the statue as well. "She's beautiful," she said quickly, even though she wasn't staring at the statue she'd painted the other day. Now it was such a trivial fact.

- And very expensive! – Merkez the maid thought about the price of such a statue.

- Oh, that's for sure! Hm! - she was still looking at the water with a worried look. - Hm! If only this crowd would disperse one day!

The maid Merkez nodded in amazement.

- Dessy, you're being strangely impatient today!

Dessy nodded her head quickly.

-Yes, yes. A little bit I did! But I think I'll get better as soon as this crowd outside comes to an end now!

And of course, the crowd with the press and the first press conference came to an end, they later treated themselves to all sorts of delicacies in the reception salon on the ground floor of that big house, they talked about trophies, about horses and the Hippodrome and it's nice to have that riding enthusiasm – because in order to have top, best, racehorses in the country, you have to be a fan of everything related to equestrian sport. Of course, the reporters went about their business and their own homes, and Dessy finally snuck out of the room, aware that it was a good thing that her beloved and beautiful marman hadn't been splashing around the water that morning with a nice, golden tail, because he would certainly have been a little more of a sensation than all Dad's horses and those expensive polished trophies in the office.

Dessy, a little relieved and more relaxed, walked towards the barn, of course she looked into the water of the old fountain, but now she couldn't see anything there. If only she could somehow make that beautiful merman come to the surface again? What an unusual and wonderful feeling it was that she had the opportunity to kiss him. A once-in-a-lifetime opportunity ," she said to herself and walked into the barn more confidently. Not every girl has the opportunity to kiss a beautiful merman in her dad's fountain in the garden. I've never kissed a man. Someone never even sees him ...

The familiar smell of fertilizer and hay blew in. All the horses stood as they normally should have stood in that stable. She calmly approached the best horse Wicky and stroked his mane and neck. The horse had always been wonderful and friendly to her, and she enjoyed that wonderful ineffable love of two completely different living beings.

-It was a fine day to-day, my dear horse! - she said in a somewhat ecstatic voice. She didn't even need to know who she was thinking about at the time.

Spidey, the blue spider that had lived in the barn for years, wonderfully encamped in the spider's web in the corner, now just retreated a little further inside so that she wouldn't notice him. It existed like this for a while, until Dessy went a little further to the other horses and gave them a little of her daily attention. Spidey the spider

moved forward again to get as close as possible to his best friend in the stable, which was the horse Wicky.

- O-O-O! I've got to take care of myself in the corner. – said Spidey the spider calmly, thinking about whether he should make another new web, which maybe wasn't so necessary for him at that moment . Although from the excess of nets, it certainly does not hurt the head. I'm going to have to stock up on who knows what the future holds. Even dust is no longer what it used to be.

- Why do you say that? - asked Wicky the horse, staring at the big blue spider in front of him.

Dessy is in the closet.

The foal Jeanna glanced briefly at Dessy, and then turned all her attention back to Spidey the spider.

- What's the matter, Spidey? They won't eat you.

- Yes, it won't. You're right, Jeanne - said Spidey the spider , coughing a little. - But I had a terrible dream last night.

- A terrible dream? - asked the foal Jeanna thoughtfully.

- What kind of dream now? It's strange that spiders dream very vividly ... – remarked Wicky the horse.

- I dreamed that Dessy and the boss Demetriso brought a hundred brooms to clean the cobwebs. All the brooms were in rainbow colors. And I dreamed that they cleaned all the cobwebs in the barn and on the property. Not a single spider survived that arduous process of cleanliness, and I got out of it by jumping into that fountain – Spidey the spider replied to his real nightmare from which he could not recover. Especially from those rainbow-colored brooms.

- Okay, okay. I don't think it's important to know all the details.

But he didn't finish everything he thought he needed to say. At that moment, Dessy again with some standard and daily boredom, came to the horse Wicky and petted him.

- So, dear Wicky, our dear horse has received a winning statue!

She then slowly untied him and took him with her to the old fountain. There was no one there now, and the fountain was somewhat embellished with a huge, white statue of a horse standing beside it. Dessy smiled, then slowly pointed towards the statue.

- Isn't this wonderful?

For a few moments, Dessy stood beside Wicky's horse and showed him this enormous statue, but this could not have touched or delighted this horse in the least, because Wicky the horse did not understand the art and benefits of modern sculpture. And while they stood in front of the fountain for a while, the other horses watched them with interest from the stable.

-And what's going on now? - asked a young foal named Koktier, who had glared at Dessy Wicky and that strange and enormous depiction of a stone horse.

- Nothing significant, - said the foal Jeanna. - Now they're looking at that big statue of Wicky the horse.

- A statue? - asked Koktier thoughtfully.

A statue that was placed next to the fountain in Wicky's honor. The boss Demetrisio wanted to repay him because Wicky has been the best horse in races at the hippodrome for a long time – the foal Jeanna explained to him patiently.

- But how will this statue help my Uncle Wicky in this tormented horse life? – again Koktier couldn 't help but ask one of his traditional stupid questions.

-Well... Not at all. It's just a sign of gratitude.

- I don't understand. Maybe I'm too young to understand. But I promise that I will definitely understand one day ... – Koktier explains his view.

And while Dessy and the horse Wicky were standing next to the old fountain, they were approached by the boss Demetrisio with a slightly faster step.

- Dessy, you're here.

- Yes, Dad. – said the one who flinched a little when she heard her father's voice behind her.

Tomorrow will be a celebration in honor of the statue. Numerous journalists from Rome will also come – he quickly explained to her what he had just arranged with representatives of some newspaper editorial offices. He wiped his forehead at it.

- Isn't that too much publicity for one horse? I mean for one statue ...

- Wicky has been racing for a long time . He wins the cup every time. He deserves to have both a statue and publicity – boss Demetrisio proudly said everything he had said in front of the media representatives a moment ago, so that he sounded to himself as if he was winded.

- I think I understand, - Dessy confirmed.

- Your fiancé Gianni will also come from Rome, - said her boss Demetrisio, almost proud of the fact

Dessy was again surprised to hear Gianni's name and that Gianni would still be coming here. She couldn't hide her amazement.

- Gianni? - But why?

Demetrisio kept looking at her, he was thoughtful.

- What – why? What kind of stupid question is that now? Dessy, that's your fiancé – he reminded me of that fact that made him even more proud. He took the reins out of her hands and rode his horse towards the stable.

- It will also be the day when everyone, including the whole of Rome, will know that you are engaged to him. Other girls would be happy about it. And you look totally indifferent to me – he said this, aware that Dessy doesn't have that cheerful enthusiasm of a young girl at all when her fiancé is mentioned. Yes, she managed to notice it, but it must have been her youthful bugs in her head that she almost had to export.

He calmly led the horse Wicky to the stable, and she was thoughtful for a few moments. She just slowly caressed the water with her palm, feeling the warmth of her heart suddenly. Feelings of true love overwhelmed her a little, and she wondered what her father would say if he knew the real truth.

- Ah, if only my father knew and suspected for whom my heart beats? At that time, no journalist would have said that I was engaged to a boring Gianni from Rome.

During this time, the Merman Fasel and the cheerful and colorful fish Miklay were under water. They stood like good friends next to each other, looking up at the surface and the vague figure of Dessy who was steadily standing upstairs.

The fish Miklay looked at Dessy's figure for a while , and then looked at the Merman Fasel.

- I have the correct impression that we haven't seen Dessy here that often today.

- Of course not, Miklay. Today they were journalists and they were taking pictures of that statue – that horse – said he, who had never been too interested in that statue, unless there was perhaps some delicious morsel on the statue, such as a sparrow or some other smaller bird. Admittedly, he was no longer a country cat, so bird specialties were no longer on his mind.

- I don't know, I've never seen that horse in the water before, - said Miklay the fish.

- On the surface, above, I saw it.

- Is it beautiful?

- An ordinary horse Wicky ... - he explained his vision to her.

- I'll try to imagine it - said Miklay the fish slowly.

- Mostly I think it's a good thing that Dessy didn't hang around the "Fountain of Wishes" – said Merman Fasel, although today's noise and crowd was certainly interesting to him. Of course, he didn't consider it controversial and obliged to peek out a little and see these journalists. He just stared at it all under the water.

- Do you still think that girl is obsessed with kissing Merman? - It would be – if I know how to count correctly – a second kiss for you, wouldn't it? – remarked the fish Miklay, who couldn't even honestly figure out what such an unusual act as a kiss looked like. It was a real noun, something like complicated laws in astronomy.

-Yes.

They swim a little further.

- What is more beautiful and better today than the fact that your dad is a rich boss Demetriso, the owner of a bank and oil platforms, when you live in a stud farm where there are top horses, you have a fiancé in Rome and, in addition, a merman in the "Fountain of Desires"? – said Merman Fasel, who of course did not consider it controversial to think about this option when he was an ordinary yellow, It's a fat cat.

- But she doesn't know that this is the "Fountain of Wishes"

Merman Fasel looked questioningly at this colorful and unusual fish, the only specimen in that underwater pond.

- Luckily he doesn't know. Do you want to find out? That would be terrible, Ribo Miklay! – Merman Fasel couldn't honestly even think of this horror. Dessy with this knowledge.

-But why?

Who knows what Dessy would have wanted. That's how the whole world is, except me. It could be a mermaid or a mythical creature. A jellyfish or a Roman goddess. Or.. Anyway, only then would she certainly not leave me alone ... They would be together day and night. She would forget about hair bands, fancy style, holes in skirts and red boots. Forget everything! I'm sure I'd have to be with her all day and night, until total madness overwhelmed me!

- You mean? – asked the fish Miklay suspiciously. He couldn't even figure out what the fancy and red boots were, but it didn't matter at all.

It's not that I think so, but I'm convinced of it.

- But I don't understand!

- You don't understand exactly – what?

Fish Miklay was a little thoughtful.

- Well, if Dessy has that fiancé, at least that's what you say ...

-Yes I do. She has a fiancé and I saw him. Feet to the ground, head on shoulders, so humanly average. He has eyes, ears, larynx, even fingernails – I'm telling you a total human average!

- Why does she keep lingering around this fountain? - it was a really clever question whose answer is unclear or somewhere in some law of astronomy that should have been studied in the very near future.

- I don't know – shook his head Merman Fasel to whom all this with Dessy and her curiosity was incomprehensible. She should be riding a horse, painting, writing poetry, combing her hair, or anything other than what she was doing in those days – staring at the water. What a spectacle – kilotons of pond water!

- Maybe she's bored, - Miklay the fish assumes.

- I don't believe it. The stud farm is very large, you can ride someone to the horse.

Finally, the fish Miklay comes to a unique conclusion and discovery that may have been the answer to all this topic about Dessy.

- Maybe he likes the smell of toadstool from this fountain.

Merman Fasel shook his head.

- Not that! She loves perfumes! I know that. I was in her room. It's certainly like a perfumery there," he said, aware that the room had never been overly interesting, too scented, clean, boring. With a bunch of perfumes, makeup, hair bands, nail polish, and all the other essentials for a young girl. It's terribly annoying!

- You know a lot about her? – remarked the fish Miklay.

Merman Fasel nodded his head quickly.

- At least as long as it took for a cat, a pet, to find out about its owner.

- Well, and even that wasn't enough for us to figure out why he was constantly fidgeting around? - concluded Miklay the fish , aware that it had already become like a big puzzle for him.

Merman Fasel, who had begun to get on his nerves with the topic of Dessy, now calmly turned to this colorful fish.

- Miklay, do me a favor!

Miklay the fish blinked in confusion.

- What?

- Stop talking about annoying Dessy. And now, come, I want to see that one underwater cave – said Merman Fasel, who was now fascinated by all the colorfulness of the underwater world to such an extent that he wanted to explore and see everything in one fell swoop, but it was impossible. Namely, the underwater lake was very large, and through some tunnels it led all the way to the exit to the sea, but there was a lot to swim there. That is why now Merman Fasel was only interested in investigating everything that, as an ordinary cat, he could not reasonably have imagined while he was on the surface and engaged in catching sparrows or mice.

3.

And in two days, of course, the boss Demetrisio organized another slightly larger and more spectacular press conference. Now he wanted to tell everyone that his only daughter, Dessy, was engaged to such a wonderful young man as Gianni from Rome. He was beautiful, rich, young, every girl's dream on this planet, he was his daughter's fiancé. Boss Demetrisio was proud of their love affair, which will now be talked about throughout the country.

Now there were a lot of journalists, and they were all in front of that old fountain in order to immortalize these grandiose moments of such a rich engagement between two young people. It's a sensation that's worth capturing with cameras for all interested readers of the yellow press.

On the roof of that house there was a large nest of two storks. They were: Tropp and Mexy. They looked with interest at the crowd that had formed around the old fotonna.

- Do you think, Mexy, it's very crowded here right now? - asked Tropp, who sat and yawned, aware that it was a bit too much to bring a bunch of loud people flashing with those cameras every other day.

Mexy the stork looked at the crowd with sincere interest.

-I think so!

Tropp yawned again and looked down, concluding that there were about a dozen more of them than yesterday. Every day there are more and more journalists.

- And they certainly didn't come here because of us?

- No, I don't think we're the stars of the night, and we're not the stars of the day, - sighed Mexy with genuine disappointment in her voice.

- That's what I think too.

- I don't think they came because of the Merman Fasel who lives in the Fountain of Wishes - it was, of course, very smart and prudent thinking.

- No – definitely not! – sighed the Tropp stork.

- But if these journalists knew that Fasel lived in a fountain, it would be a spectacular world discovery! - said the stork Mexy and only then did he notice that no matter how much they flew to and fro, sometimes even kilometers away, they never had the opportunity to see a merman. Admittedly, they never looked too closely. Their only interest in the water was to catch a small fish and fill their stomachs with it.

- I'm completely in agreement with that. They're here for that statue of Wicky or for that engagement.

- Wicky is the best horse in the whole stud farm and has been for a long time.

-Yes! Let's take a look at all the events now! – And the two storks, filled with standard bird curiosity, flew to a tree where they very conveniently hid in the treetops from where they could follow the events.

Now everyone's eyes were on the stage. There stood the boss Demetrisio, Gianni and Dessy. Then the worker Salikil came on stage. There was a big round of applause.

- It is our pleasure and honor to present you the statue of the horse Wicky. Wicky is our best, most beautiful, strongest and fastest horse. For those of you who haven't been here a few days ago

Dessy, who didn't like the fact that it was so crowded here again, kept fidgeting on one leg. She didn't want her father to make her engagement to Gianni public. And she liked it even less that it was with all the fuss and noise, all next to the fountain where her beloved dear merman was , who could see it all, of course, only if he was interested and if he looked a little closer. At the same time, she realized that she would never be able to win him over in the way she might have wanted, and that drove her to despair. But now wasn't the time to be desperate.

Especially not in front of a crowd of curious photojournalists and well-known city journalists.

- That horse Wicky is all the best - she said in a whisper, leaning towards her fiancé, Gianna, who was much taller than her, so he only looked at her briefly.

- And mostly - the worker Salikil continued his presentation - we thank the workers who worked on the installation of this statue, the sculptor who sculpted this statue, as well as all of you who want to see off these beautiful moments.

Then Dessy and Gianni gave each other a nice but somewhat artificial smile and stepped forward.

Down in the water were the merman Fasel and the fish Miklay, who were watching the muffle up there with interest. They saw Gianni and Dessy on stage as they stepped forward and smiled at each other

If I were an ordinary orange cat, I'd be watching this whole thing from a discreet distance. Somewhere, from a tree or a fence ... – said Merman Fasel, who at the moment did not regret those ordinary, cat days at all.

- I have no idea what a fence or a tree looks like - remarked Miklay, the fish, who didn't even know what those words meant.

- Don't worry, Fish Miklay, you haven't missed anything big!

He smiled at that.

At that time, the old fountain was still a media buzz. Flashes were lit up, and everyone commented that the young couple Gianni and Dessy were made for each other. Gianni looked at Dessy's reflection in profile and smiled. It seemed as if he was in love with her.

- Dessy!

Dessy glanced at him, trying to get into the role of a girl in love.

- Tell me, Gianni!

Gianni scratched his head briefly. It seemed as if he had something to give her. He gave her a real accusatory look, because he really felt a little tricked by her not answering his letters. Really weird girl. It was probably because she was spoiled by a real rich life – the young man sadly concluded.

- You have not replied to any of my letters. I've been waiting for your letter for two weeks, but ...

Dessy sighs deeply. She looked for a moment at the water and the water lilies that were there. Ah, if all this fuss had already passed! She was confused. He noticed her confusion.

-Well...

Gianni shrugged.

- I don't know... It looks like you're starting to forget me.

Dessy smiles. Of course, he couldn't even imagine how much truth there was in his words. Indeed, if the maid Merkez hadn't shaken her out of that state of total infatuation with Gianni's letter, Dessy wouldn't have remembered that she had a fiancé.

- No, I...- she shook her head.

- You are becoming indifferent, admit it.

Dessy knew that she now had to get out of the new situation very smartly. Gianni could have guessed something, to do some research, to ask her to come to Rome. The thought now seemed monstrous to her. You have to come up with something smart – she said to herself – now you have to lie convincingly!

-No! Rather, we were all busy preparing about... eye.. around the statue. This is a very big event for our stud farm "Demetriso", you know that!

-Okay! – he spoke in a more conciliatory tone. – But see that you will write to me a little more often soon.

Photojournalists took a lot of pictures of the people who were on the stage, and Merman Fasel and Miklay the fish patiently watched it underwater all the time.

The next day, the pictures were published in the daily newspapers. The headlines were identical: "Rich boss Demetrisio betrothed his daughter to young Gianni". And people gathered around the newsstands to buy newspapers and read all that was written about them. Even the landlord Demetirisio took several different newspapers to read all that had been written about him and his sweetheart, perfectly happy to have betrothed his daughter to such an extraordinary young man, and that the engagement now reverberated throughout Italy, Or maybe even part of Europe. As Demetrisio was a prominent banker and oil magnate, this meant that many people in European business circles were now aware that he was engaged to his daughter. And that also meant that many young men who might have hoped to be Dessy's fiancés now have no chance of doing so.

And so this engagement was the main news of the day in Italy.

4.

The next morning dawned beautiful, beautiful and sunny. The blue sky was dotted with a few beautiful little white clouds. Birds were singing in the trees, two storks were calmly observing the situation, and everything was going on in the usual morning routine.

Dessy slept peacefully. Perhaps she had something interesting, but that, dear children, we do not want to disturb you now. Slowly the young girl woke up stretching out on that beautiful bed in the lovely girl's room. Through the window she could see part of the blue sky and the clouds that were dotted.

- Today I may see him again! Oh! – she said it in a cheerful tone, perfectly aware that her sweet little secret was the best thing she had this summer. Again, in her scattered thoughts, she revived his figure, hating the fact that she didn't want to pee into that fountain to see him a little better.

It is not nice, she said to herself convincingly, to run after a man, and especially not to jump into that fountain for him. The most important thing is to be and stay nice.

Dessy then slowly stood up, combed her hair, hummed it, and danced for a short time. A few minutes later, in a cheerful tone, she walked down the stairs. The maid Merkez watched in amazement for a few moments, and then Dessy, with a few bars on the piano, stepped out of the water and walked over to the fountain.

She looked left to right and saw that she was alone in the garden.

- Ah good! Well, there is no one – no one!

Then she finally leaned over the "Fountain of Wishes" and looked into the water without noticing anything special, except for a few small fish that swam there and who had never been interested in her.

- Whoa! Merman! Beautiful, merman, are you here? – she touched the water with her hand, wishing that she could touch him with such a simple movement of her palm. But that was now completely impossible.

Meanwhile, the Merman Fasel, the fish Miklay, and the Serpent were standing down in the water . For a few moments they stared questioningly at the surface, at the figure of a young, idle girl who was touching the water and saying something.

- Is this her... she... – asked the Serpent, trying to remember again what the young girl's name was.

Merman Fasel looked again at the surface and at the female figure above, which seriously disturbed the idyll of water harmony. As if he was a little bored with Dessy's constant persistent presence, he just sighed deeply.

- Dessy - he replied.

The snake smiled.

- Yes, Dessy.

Merman Fasel looked at the Serpent, and then looked up again at the annoying girl above. He pursed his lips angrily.

- Her name is Desdemona.

-But why does everyone call her Dessy? - asked the Serpent.

-Because no one calls her Desdemona - replied Merman Fasel, who had always been a little frightened by the name, without even knowing why it was so.

- People often come up with nicknames, don't they? - remarked Miklay, the fish, who had now become quite accustomed to the fact that Dessy would be up all the time, at least during the day, and that it was nothing unusual anymore. Perhaps the girl still wanted to come to terms with the fate of that monument of the horse above... There's something about that horse inspiration. Moments of horse inspiration should be preserved.

-Well, yes... how when . .. how to whom ...

- She's going to spend all her time by this fountain every day now - the Serpent remarked, the generally clear fact of Dessy's constant presence.

- And they'll keep looking at the water - said Miklay the fish , who then thought that it must be fun to be up there, while the bright summer sun scorched you, staring at the water. A spectacular feeling that you will never even experience.

- I don't think she can see us here.

- And it can't. She's a man - said Merman Fasel, who seemed delighted with the fact that, well, she wore that skirt with puffs and boots and didn't have a tail like him.

-What you mean? - The Serpent asked.

- Well, it's obvious that it's not a cat . . . – said Merman Fasel vaguely.

-I don't understand. And why should it be a cat? – asked Miklay the fish, pouting his mouth as he did so. He was aware that there was a world up there that he did not know, and that he would never have the opportunity to know.

- Cats are very good at seeing. A cat's eyesight is almost like a camera – replied Merman Gianni, aware that it might be something he was missing from the cat world.

- Fasel, but you don't have that sight anymore here! – said the fish Miklay and stared into the eyes of Merman Fasel, trying to figure out what that cat's eyesight looked like.

- No! - said Merman Fasel, waving his hand at that. "Now I can see very well... but as a man... I mean like a fish. It's like Merman. Dessy doesn't see us now.

Everyone was relieved when he said that. He was still looking at the surface, and Dessy, who was still standing there like some beautiful fashion threat.

- But she is very persistent in the fact that she may be supervising us a little or...

- She could stick her head under water. Then she would surely see us... – the Serpent remarked, trying to imagine this new horror in the fountain with Dessy's head lurking at any moment.

Merman Fasel shook his head.

- I hope he doesn't do that. Besides, we would have run away, she wouldn't have noticed us. Other than that, she won't do it.

Miklay the fish popped his mouth again thoughtfully.

- Are you sure of that?

Merman Fasel nodded his head.

- One hundred percent. That way she would ruin her curls and expensive hairband. Maybe she would lose one of the earrings as well? She's so cute and fancy.

The snake sighed deeply.

- Fancy?

Fish Miklay enthusiastically notices something that has been perfectly clear since he was born, but he has only now become aware of it .

- I've got a sneak peek on my body too. Do you think I'm fancy too?

- It's classy, fashionable, and popular. And you, Fish Miklay, you're just a fish – replied Merman Fasel calmly and looked at those unusual fish patterns. – You're not classy, and you don't follow the new fashion in Paris ...

- Yes, I really suck because I don't follow fashion in Paris.

Aware that the girl up there would still be there all day, they calmly swam towards the caves.

- Basically, it's about the fact that Dessy is here all the time, and we fish, snakes and the rest of the aquatic gang don't feel as solid and relaxed as we used to. We are not happy, and we don't have peace either – said the Snake, who seemed to have publicly said everything that everyone was already thinking.

- Water peace? – asked Miklay the fish thoughtfully.

- And my level of water harmony has been exceeded! – said Merman Fasle , who was thinking about the level of water harmony at that time and that he no longer had the patience for that boredom up there.

Fish Miklay was even more pensive.

- Water harmony? I didn't even know that there was a level of harmony.

Merman Fasel almost felt better when they clung to one of those beautiful caves. Of course, some of the harmony has been restored. Maybe he should move permanently to one of those caves, at least he would be completely calm there.

- Everything and water was wonderful, beautiful; We could sing nicely during the day, if she hadn't accidentally grabbed me and kissed me.

- Yes - exclaimed Miklay the fish. - I agree with that. That kiss was crucial!

- We used to have those three boring fat catfish, and now we have a fancy Dessy. – said the Snake, remembering those three fat big catfish, which at one time were a real fear and trembling for all the inhabitants of the old fountain. – We are on the same page again, but in a different package.

- This is a fancy, fancy package now - said Miklay the fish.

Then they swam out again from that cave that they had seen several times and which was smaller and not very interesting. Now they swam back to the middle from where they saw that Dessy, of course, was up there.

-Yes, and that fancy package is about to jump in here and catch Merman Fasel - said the Serpent, trying to imagine the impossible horror that almost threatened to become a real reality.

- Does that girl up there have any other interests? - asked Miklay, trying to create for his little fish brain a picture of the world up there, which seemed strange, strange, distant...

- He has horses, a hippodrome, fashion magazines, weekly shopping, a fiancé to whom he has to write even though he certainly does not do it, he has a garden, storks, animals - agreed Merman Fasel calmly. He knew some of his landlady's routines, although he never poked his nose too much into all these things because they didn't concern him. However, it was more important to see where his cat food was, whether the pantry door might be open, whether there was a mouse nearby, and where he could get a nice and cultured cat sleep.

- Okay, all right - replied Miklay the fish.

- You don't have to go into detail! - replied the Serpent.

- And now he only has this Fountain of Wishes - remarked the fish Miklay. I'm sure Dessy had this one a year ago, but it wasn't that boring.

- And the dream of Fasel merman. And I'm Fasel, almost one hundred percent sure that she's about 300 percent in love with you," the Snake said of his clever snake observation. Because there is some truth in the fact that snakes can distinguish the signature of reptiles. It's like a real version of a snake's reflection in a mirror: they recognized themselves and could sense anything and everything. The snake sensed the girl's feelings upstairs, not knowing whether it might be right for her to start feeling sorry for her so nicely.

- And I wanted so much to be a merman, to wander around and enjoy the harmony of the best frog orchestra in the world! And nothing! – said Merman Fasel and looked briefly at the gold coins at the bottom. Now the possibility of awakening the Water Spirit was utterly impossible.

- Maybe it's not too late to be a cat again - the Serpent remarked calmly. And she could have guessed it, that the Merman Fasel would surely be as calm as a fat cat now. "There's some beauty in the hair, too."

- And in the tail!

- And only in its claws - said the Serpent calmly.

- I hate fleas! - replied Merman Fasel, who really never liked to scratch and scribble, and even less so when Dessy powdered him with some horrible flea powder that would make him really sick for the next three days.

- Well? What is it—a flea? - asked the Serpent, imagining this strange creature in the style of a flea as something really delightful. Even the name 'flea" sounded very wonderful to her.

- That's why I would never want to be an ordinary cat from a stud farm again.

And while they were standing down there talking about it all, a cute little frog named Mila calmly swam up to them.

- Hello company! – said the frog Mila, standing next to them, and then she noticed that they were looking up towards the surface of the water. Almost everyone in that fountain has been doing that a lot lately, so it wasn't something unusual even now. Who do we have here? She's the girl up there, isn't she?

- And it will be there . . . . - sighed the Serpent. –Hours...

Mila the frog, who, of course, in the style of any frog, could jump to the surface of the water and sit on a leaf of water lilies, had already seen many people and the world up on the surface, but it was not so interesting to her.

She's the strangest human being I've ever seen.

-She's in love with Fasel - the Serpent remarked.

The little frog sighed.

-Yes. And what to do with it?

That's why he's here! – said the Serpent

- How strange! If I were a girl, I would certainly never stand there for hours staring at an old "Fountain of Wishes". Incomprehensible! – that's what she really meant sincerely.

- Don't worry, dear frog. I'm convinced that Dessy and her father can't understand, let alone the best frog orchestra in the world in the Old Fountain of Wishes - replied Merman Fasel, aware that it would be a few more weeks before Dessy went somewhere again in the autumn , and by then his water harmony would be at a dead end.

They then stared up at Dessyn's figure next to the fountain for a while. During this time, the figure of the landlord Demetrisio appeared at the window of the house. He had been looking at the fountain in the room for some time, and Dessy was standing there looking at the water. He was amazed at her new habit. Meanwhile, the hard-working maid Merkez was tidying up the room a little, not paying any attention to what was happening outside.

- Merkez! - said the landlord Demetrisio suddenly.

The hard-working maid Merkez paused a bit at that moment. She looked at him for a moment. He knew that something was going on outside of his mind.

-Tell me, Mr. Demetrisio.

She then slowly and steadily walked over to the window and looked at Dessy and the fountain. Both older people were surprised by Dessy's new habit – complete confusion next to that fountain.

-What do you think? Is there anything unusual about my daughter standing next to that fountain for hours? - He asked, a little worried. He looked at the maid for a moment, and then at his daughter again. He smoothed his gray moustache in confusion.

- Maybe it relaxes her! Or admire the statue of the horse Wicky. - It's probably Boss Demetrisio - she said calmly. Girl after girl had some unusual inclinations, but many young people today had a variety of inclinations and interests. Aware that the scene outside was quite monotonous and that it would certainly be so in the coming period – she calmly went on and continued with her work.

Boss Demetrisio stared at his daughter for a while, then slowly adjusted the buttons on his plaid work shirt.

He then came to his desk where a daily mail, newspapers and some documents were waiting for him, which he had to sign and send to one of the banks.

-I hope it's as you think! - he said in a somewhat worried tone, unable to decipher what was happening to his daughter now.

Of course, an older and smart man would certainly be extremely shocked to find out and discover that there is a beautiful meran with a golden tail in that fountain, with which she fell in love at first sight. But maybe it was only a matter of time before he would find out and what could really happen to Merman Fasel then?

In the end, a little more thoughtful, the boss Demetrisio decided to go to Dessy's room for a short time. He opened the door and saw several of Gianni's letters that were on the table. He approached them and noticed that she hadn't even opened them. They were completely intact. He snorted angrily. This bothered him deeply and he knew that he would really have to do something about it .

5.

During this time, Dessy's faithful Gianni spent his days in Rome. He lived in a beautiful and wealthy neighborhood, in an apartment where he had everything his heart wished for and what his parents could afford. His father was a lawyer and his mother was a doctor and an art lover. So through her, Gianni liked to visit museums and started working as a curator.

He loved art, nature and walking. He had a new car, but he preferred to walk or ride a bike.

Gianni was very tall, had broad shoulders, bright eyes and short light brown hair. He always wore elegant and expensive clothes, used expensive men's perfumes, and was just as fancy as Dessy. And he met her at a fashion show that spring, when the boss Demetrisio decided that now was the right time for Dessy to have a fiancé. And the young smart Gianni seemed like the right choice to him.

And all this would have been ideal, of course, if Gianni, as a young man, had not written all those wonderful romantic letters to his fiancée to which she did not respond. So in those days he was already wondering if she had received those letters and if she had read them. It was extremely strange behavior for a young and beautiful girl.

On that day, some of his old acquaintances came to visit him. So in the drawing room , where the walls were cheerful blue and expensive white furniture, there were now Prince Angust and Denny. They were sitting on the sofa and watching Gianni as he stood in front of the window looking out into the street.

Rome was warm and bathed in sunlight that day. People walked the streets and went to work. And he had a day off that day, which he decided to share with old acquaintances.

Prince Angust did not live in Italy, but he had been visiting Rome for two weeks with his young wife, Princess Bernadette. He also visited an old friend of his, who complained to him about the behavior of his fiancée Dessy. Prince Angust had long blond hair that he kept tied up in a ponytail, and now he wore more casual summer clothes.

Denny glanced at Prince Angust for a moment, and then turned his attention back to Gianni.

-So a letter? - said Denny.

-I'm writing to my fiancée, Dessy - Gianni said, turning to them.

Prince Angust then raised his eyebrows ironically.

- But she didn't even answer your previous three letters.

Gianni shakes her head.

- No, he's not!

- And you're writing to her again?

Gianni glanced at him for a moment, and then at Dessy's framed picture on the table.

- They had a lot of fuss about that statue of their best horse on the estate, so she didn't have time to answer - he tried to give a somewhat clever answer.

Prince Angust sighed deeply. The young man seemed to be in a state of disbelief, which was very clearly and concretely maintained on his face at that moment.

- I hope it is as you say! - said Prince Angust, who could not have imagined that today a pretty girl would pay more attention to an ordinary racehorse than to her fiancé from Rome. But today everything is possible.

- Now it will be different! I told her that it was time for her to get back to normal and respond to my dogs.

Prince Angust was surprised again.

- But what kind of girl is she when you need to remind her of the usual and usual things? – And the three young men spent that afternoon talking about how some girls today don't know how to appreciate romance at all.

Later, when he saw off his good two friends and was left all alone, the young man Gianni thought about what they were talking about.

For a moment, he almost gave up on the idea of being cultured and considerate enough to write another letter for Dessy. But then, still carried by beautiful emotions, he sat down at his desk and began to write:

"Dear Dessy,

Today I spent the day in wonderful conversations with my friends that I told you about. They were Prince Angust and my old acquaintance Denny. We talked about the benefits of love and making friends. The day was filled with wonderful productive conversations.

I wish you could be here in Rome now, visiting all the museums, interesting places, restaurants and parks. I wish we could walk on beautiful warm evenings and look forward to the sunset that comes every day ... There is not much we can do now, except to send a few letters to each other. I would rejoice in your kind words and the fact that you are happy that the days will finally come when we will be together forever.

I think of you every day

Your fiancé Gianni"

And he slowly folded the paper into an envelope and wrote the address. The next morning, when he was on his way to work at the City Museum, where he had been working since nine in the morning, he just stopped by the post office and sent the letter.

The courier postal service worked very perfectly every day, so that already that evening the letter for Dessy was in the mail car . The next day, the diligent postman took the letter with all the postal documents all the way to the place where Dessy lived. The letter ended up in the hands of the maid Merkez, who again brought the letter on a silver platter , squirming so beautifully and sympathetically. Again, Dessy paid a little more attention to her hair and hairband, sang a little more and looked longingly at the fountain. And the maid Merkez, of course, did what she had done with all of Gianni's letters up to that point – she just put it on the table among all those envelopes. As she walked out of Dessy's room, the maid Merquez couldn't help but wonder when the young man would get tired of writing to this impossible girl who pays more attention to frogs and water lilies than to anything resembling romance.

And the frogs didn't seem romantic at all , did they?

On that day, Dessy thought for a long time about everything that was happening in her life now. She would only glance briefly and seldom at the Gianni letters on the table, which were piling up neatly, though neither of them ever had any strong desire to open and possibly read a little of what her fiancé had written to her.

Why should a girl read the letters her fiancé writes to her at all today, she wondered calmly as she sat and drew the figure of her beloved Merman Fasel in a scrapbook?Really a lot of things from today's girls – she concluded calmly and completely calmly.

Especially in her case, because that love romance and relationship with Gianni was not something Dessy wanted. It had been arranged by her father, and it was something that had been imposed and loaded upon her, just as all kinds of overweight loads are always neatly loaded onto mules, and she still felt a little stupid about this relationship. No one asked her if she loved her. No one asked her if she had any feelings for him. He was like an obligation to her, which she had to obey somehow, although she herself could not think of their wedding at the moment, where she, in white and with a bouquet in her hands, would go to Gianni for a wonderful, idyllic life for all times and for all occasions.

She almost shuddered at the thought, as if she were rushing into some serious incurable infectious disease that would surely completely mow her down. She began to think about her merman, and about the fact that she had seen it quite by chance, and that it was perhaps the most beautiful fact in the whole story. It was not imposed on her. He only swam and splashed in that fountain over there, now eternally hidden in those depths so that she could never see him, reach him, kiss him...

Love was born completely by accident, although admittedly quite one-sided, but it doesn't matter. The important thing is that she has experienced something so beautiful and unusual, and that it is the most beautiful value of all. All the loves that are so sudden are sure to live forever, and if nothing else, Dessy was now quite convinced that she would never forget him.

And she finished drawing her Merman Fasel. As she was a good painter, the painting was very convincing and she looked longingly at him, trying to decipher since he had been in that fountain, why had she never seen him before ? Is it the only one like this, or are there more? And how could she see and discover it now? She doesn't know how to swim very well, and who knows how much she can swim? She never found out. I'm just going to go to that old fountain. Now all this had a completely different symbolism and significance.

She looked at the figure of Merman Fasel in her scrapbook for a few more moments, and then she locked the scrapbook and left it in a drawer. She didn't want her father or, for example, the maid Merkez to find out about Merman's existence.

What seemed even worse to her in those moments was that she only now realized that she knew nothing about him, only that she lived in that fountain. But still, the significance of his existence was quite enough for her. Everything else seemed superfluous in the eyes of the young girl.

And of course, the following week, three good friends reunited at Gianni's apartment. The theme was again the same – Gianni's unusual love problems. For he seemed to be the only young man in Rome, and perhaps in all of Italy and Europe, who had a problem of this kind.

Now young Denny was standing in front of a large patio window, from where there was a view of the Roman Cathedral as if in a beautiful watercolor painting . A multitude of pigeons flew around, and the sky was clear blue and cloudless. The day was as hot and humid as summer days can be.

Denny, who was standing there, turned abruptly to the two men who were sitting quietly watching him.

-Well, Gianni! - said Denny.

-Tell me, Danny! - replied Gianni, who was thinking again that day of Dessy and of the fact that he had not received an adequate answer to any of the letters he had sent . But he had a small little hope, that at some point some answer would surely come from the estate, and that he should not despair much.

Denny stretched out and looked at his best friend worriedly.

- I was right!

-Right about what? - asked Gianni.

Denny then sat down on a beautiful armchair that fit perfectly into the ambience of the room.

- When I said three weeks ago that we would see if Dessy would answer you.

-That's what I said - Prince Angust reminded them. - What kind of girl is she when she needs to be reminded of that? - Prince Angust was sitting across from them on the sofa. He looked, now and then at another, somehow sinking into these thoughts that Dessy was really the strangest girl in the world.

-No! - replied Gianni in a somewhat sad tone. Somehow, in the grayness of waiting for an answer from her, the will and desire to develop a romance has passed. He was a little angry with her because she really neglected him. And if nothing else, at least with a relationship with her, he would have wonderful contacts in the world of her father's business, banking empire, which was no small thing at all.

- Not a single letter, and there were at least seven of them ...

- Maybe she's sick - Denny remarked, though that possibility seemed a little impossible in the middle of a beautiful summer.

- Although I'm sure she would have written at least one letter even then. Girls in times of colds – especially emotional – Gianni said of his current statement.

- Gianni, I have to admit that Danny is right - said Prince Angust.

- She's so strange!

- Who knows what she's interested in now! - remarked Prince Angust, for it was utterly impossible that he would devote more attention to some horses than to romance with his fiancé all summer. - I understand that your engagement was wanted by Master Demetrisio, but...

Then Gianni, somehow gloomy, got up and went to the window. He looked outside with a blank and slightly sad look. It was as if some of his beautiful emotions were slowly subsiding and disappearing, and it was as if he was not yet strong enough to admit it to himself.

- I'll wait a while longer, and then I'll have to talk to her very seriously .

- Yes, Giani, that's right.

Prince Angust had almost begun to feel sorry for his best friend, but he tried not to show it quite openly. Gianni was a very proud and proud young man.

- Because this is how you look like some romantic sufferer

Prince Angust only smiled at this observation, and Gianni turned and looked at him questioningly.

It was the role he least wanted.

6.

The day at the estate of the landlord Demetrisio began in the usual course. Everything took place according to a fixed and orderly schedule to which everyone – people, animals – was very accustomed. Order, work, and discipline were what were valued among the workforce that was there.

The weather was excellent, even such a wonderful morning that Mila the frog and Rinnie the toad came out to the surface of the water. They settled down very comfortably and comfortably on the large leaves of the water lily, where they croaked, until they saw, of course, none other than Dessy hurriedly approaching them.

When the young girl had reached the fountain, she stopped and stared into the water, and the two frogs were watching her calmly with a routine question mark. Not long after, they noticed that the old fountain was approaching with hurried steps and the owner Demetrisio, who came out of the barn, wiped his hands first on an old cloth and came to his daughter. Questionably , he stared at the water, the water lilies and the flowers, and then he stared at his daughter with an even bigger question mark on his face than Mila the frog and Rinnie the toad might have.

- And you, young girl, spend all your free time in front of this old fountain. Let's see what's interesting about it. – he looked questioningly at the water with such an expression on his face that the young girl was a little frightened. It seemed as if her father was a little angry. – Water lilies, water lily leaves, 2-3 frogs, a few flies, a bee... – he put his hands on his hips and stared at his daughter.

She shrugged her shoulders quickly. You have to be smart and not distract yourself, she told herself. The last thing she needs now is for her marman to float to the surface and wash her golden tail a little. Dessy smiled.

- It's a beautiful day!

Have you seen what I've got here?

Dessy looked at him. She didn't care what her father had to show her, but she didn't want to show it.

-What?

Meanwhile, they were staring at two frogs sitting on a water lily. They saw when the landlord Demetrisio pulled Gianni's letters out of his pocket.He looked at the letters, and then looked at his daughter.

-Letters!

She seemed a little disappointed. Maybe she would be more happy with a fashion brochure?

-Letters!

- These are Gianni's letters.

He then walked up to her, and you could see how the older man was conceived. It was a very unusual situation to which he did not know how to respond adequately. Dessy wasn't too interested in that conversation now. Ah, how her dad just now doesn't know how to go to a bank and have fun there with some fun things like numbers. Money was one of his favorite things that he knew very well.

- Yes, they are.

She nodded, staring at the letters, hoping that her father would not now fall into some crazy temptation to open one of the letters and start reading.

- That's his handwriting! - said Dessy, after taking a letter and recognizing the handwriting of her fiancé from Rome.

- You haven't written anything for Gianni for days - sighs the boss Demetrisio. He looked as if he was passing it on to her.

Dessy, however, could not hide her surprise now.

- How do you know?

- The maid Merkez told me. You know that she is the one who is in charge of taking your letters to the post office ... But your letters are gone! He's staring at her. And the whole situation was now very carefully and faithfully monitored by the two frogs on the water lily in order to inform the merman Fasel about everything. They were, after all, faithful spies, although they never sounded the trumpet about it.

- Are you stalking me? - asked Dessy in surprise. She put her hands on her hips and almost felt like smiling. But she didn't smile. Who knows how her father would have understood that. "That's not nice, Dad.

At that moment, however, Demetrisio felt a little unusual.

- I'm not stalking you, I just noticed that you ... This... Gianni doesn't care. I'm sorry, but you're spending all your free time here in front of this old fountain of wishes. I'd think you're going to have to add a gold coin every day, but I doubt that's your preoccupation at the moment.

Dessy coped better faster. She pointed to the beautiful white statue of Wicky the horse that was still standing there.

- I'm a fan of the Wicky Horse.

- It's been three weeks since you snatched it. I don't know what you're learning about this picture, but... I'm going to have to write to your fiancé, Gianni. I know this is the relationship I contracted. He is such a wonderful, smart, hardworking, rich guy from a wonderful family that ... – he tried to explain it all to her nicely, the way parents who love their impossible, stubborn and often disobedient children do.

- Dad!

- Say, Dessy!

- If I tell you that I'm going to write to him soon, will that promise reassure you a little?" she asked quickly, even though she knew she was lying to him. It's not nice to lie to your parents, but now she really didn't know how to get out of that situation.

He calmly approached her, hugged her and kissed her on the forehead.

-Wants! But write to him!

He then walked quickly into the house, but he could not help but turn around once more.

- I'm just thinking of your good Dessy. I want you to know that.

- I know, Dad. And thank you!

A few minutes later, Dessy watched as he entered the house. She sighed deeply, for the first time that morning, wishing she had a friend here on the estate that she could confide in. Now all her friends were at home in other cities. She could only write them a letter, but Dessy doubted that any of them would understand her about falling in love with an unknown merman in her fountain, and that she was completely fighting a romance with such a wonderful young man as Gianni.

And while Dessy was thinking it was time to talk to someone and confide in her feelings about the mysterious creature in the fountain, Mila the Frog and Rinnie the Toad jumped into the water. They were real witnesses of this unusual conversation, which they had to convey beautifully – word for word – to Merman Fasel.

- I think we should inform Merman Fasel about this conversation - said Milla the Frog, wondering why Dessy didn't focus on her fiancé after all, instead of staring into a water lily all day, expecting Merman Fasel, who, of course, wouldn't appear in front of her again.

The two frogs looked around and saw that apart from the fish and a couple of idle snakes, there was no one else in the middle. The goldfinches were now squeezing a little bit under the bright sun, down there in the depths, and the frogs were quickly heading for one of the caves where Merman Fasle liked to spend his time, although there was nothing interesting there, even if he had been there a couple of times.

- Do you have an interesting idea in mind, Frog Mila?

-Yes I do. Fasel keeps saying – and for three weeks, every day, how he misses peace and water harmony! – said Mila the frog, who understood the feelings of this unusual golden-tailed merman. Everyone would get bored if some rich daddy's daughter was watching him up there.

-Yes I do. And that bearable level of water harmony.what is life in a pond like when you can't be water-harmonious?

- I think I know how to somehow inform that fiancé Gianni in Rome about the real reason for Dessy's lack of care for him – although it seemed like a real treacherous act, it was the only and right solution.

- But then we will be real plaintiffs!

- Never mind. The main thing is that Fasel has that wonderful peace and water harmony again

And thinking about how to finally free themselves from Dessy and her presence, they swam to the caves.

The underwater caves were really spectacular in some places. The water in them was crystal clear, and in some places beautiful light effects were created from the crystal stones . The sun's rays that were breaking through were like an unusual light, which gave everything an extraordinary atmosphere.

Now there was a real conversation about how to restore water harmony in that fountain. And of course, the discussion was fierce. Water harmony in any degree now seemed like a distant and unattainable goal, which they would never be able to attain in that fountain. Except to wait until the fall and for Dessy to go somewhere where her father has already decided to send her for a few long months.

- So, if I understand correctly, and I think I understand the whole issue correctly - we should write to the address of this fiancé Gianni in Rome and inform him that this is not just an ordinary old fountain, but a magical "Fountain of Wishes", that the Merman Fasel with whom Dessy is in love lives here ? – concluded the toad Rinnie, who everyone thought was right the clever mistress of all the reptiles in that fountain, because she was the oldest of them all and at the same time the wisest.

-Exactly! – confirmed Mila the frog quickly.

- It's the only clever solution to restore the lost harmony - said Rinnie the toad.

- We have a few unexpected problems with this idea.

- And what are they? – asked the frog Mila.

- We don't know the address of this fiancé Gianni in Rome; first of all, the only thing we know is what Gianni looks like. And secondly, we don't even know where that fancy Rome is – said Miklay the fish, who noticed that in the last few days he had learned a number of new interesting things, such as words such as – fancy, red boots, Rome, hair bands and perfumes, wood and fences, without having any idea what it looked like, or how he could imagine it. Admittedly, what he liked most now was the word – fancy – without even knowing why it was so.

- At least that's not a problem! - said Rinnie the toad very cleverly.

- How is that not a problem? - asked Merman Fasel, who just thought that it was really an insurmountable problem now.

- There are those hated storks: Tropp and Mexy, they are migratory birds, although they live here all the time – and for free. They've seen half the world, and then they certainly know where Rome is – Rinnie the toad quickly explained, because logically if you're a migratory, and a boring gluttonous stork, then logically you've seen Rome.

- They might be able to find the address of that Gianni ... Of course, if they want to – said Mila the frog quickly, who never thought of such an interesting and clever idea.

- And if they don't eat us in time while we explain the whole issue to them - explained Rinnie the toad, whose last thing she wanted that day was to end up on the menu of those two feathered boredoms on the sidewalk.

- That's a great idea! - said Merman Fasel.

- Exactly! I agree with that! – said the fast Snake, who couldn't wait for everything to become somehow settled again and for them to be pulled out of those caves in which, because of Dessy, they had spent too much time.

- And what is the other problem? - asked Rinnie the toad.

- Well, the question is whether this fiancé Gianni is interested in everything about the fact that this is not an ordinary fountain, but a magical, fancy "Fountain of Wishes" - said the fish Miklay.

- And why shouldn't he be interested? Well, his fiancée Dessy spends almost the whole day here, I mean all her free time – Rinnie notices the toad.

- Exactly! She would be here even more – confirmed the frog Mila.

- Maybe he wants to discover the true possibilities of this magical "Fountain of Wishes" - Rinnie the toad assumes. She'd already tried to imagine him jumping into that fountain and dealing with the Fasel marman, or taking Dessy somewhere she'd never be able to find out.

- Do you think he will become the new merman?

- Two mermans in the fountain? - The snake almost froze at this observation. - Well, in that case, Dessy won't move anywhere from here. He'll want to sleep there, too.

- I'm going to get an opponent, and she's sure to order the maid Merquez to move the bed here by the Fountain.- In this way, she will be present at all times of the day and night, so that she does not miss anything new. I'm going to squirm. I'm feeling like I'm under the hood anyway.

Rinnie the toad patiently stared at him for the next few moments.

- And what is the third problem?

Fish Miklay sighs deeply.

- Yes I do! This is the third problem and this is the most complicated option right now ...

Rinnie was very interested.

- And what is it about?

-Yes, yes! Tell! Now almost all of us are really interested in tackling all these problems – confirms the frog Mila and finds out that they have long been caught up in all the problems, and there have never been too many of them.

- Exactly! We agree! It's time to restore the normal level of water harmony of this lovely pond – said Merman Fasel.

- We are fish ... Okay, we're not all fish, but we belong to the aquatic world – Miklay the fish answered.

-Really? And? – asked Merman Fasle.

- Be a little more specific - said Mila the frog.

- None of us know how to write - replied Miklay the fish.

Merman Fasel smiled at this unusually clever observation, because it is logical that no fish went to spelling and literature classes today.

- That's not true! - said Merman Fasel quickly.

- How is it not true? Did you know?

- No! - said Merman Fasel. He had seen as a cat many of Dessy's fashion magazines and a few newspapers that the boss Demetrisio had, but he never considered it controversial that a cat was messing with those headlines there.

- But I know someone who knows for sure - said Merman Fasel.

- I can tell you that we are completely fancy illiterates here! – remarked the fish Miklay.

- I see, but I think the blue spider Spidey can help us - said Merman Fasel, almost proud of the fact that he knew that the spider had always been close to all those groomers who kept a record of everything in the horse records, so Spidey had learned to read a little. And so he was always bored, so he engaged in this interest to pass the time.

- Spidey? Spidey the blue spider that lives in the corner of the barn in its wonderful dust and cobwebs? Maybe cobwebs make creatures smarter ... – Miklay the fish remarked.

Everyone in that beautiful glittering cave now seemed to disbelieve Fasel's words. Everything seemed possible, except for Spidey's well-read.

-Yes. He could help us – said Merman Fasel.

- But how? - asked the fish Miklay, confused.

- Well, first, let's say that Mila the frog or Rinnie the toad goes to the stable with the horses.

- Uh! I don't like horses... and fertilizer ... – the frog Mila was horrified at the very thought of those horses, their heads, manes, legs and everything else ...

- This is for the benefit of water harmony - Rinnie the toad reminds her.

- Yes, my dear, it's now or never. That's 5 minutes of inhaling the smell of manure.

- And maybe a horse will poop on me while I'm there! - said the frog Mila, imagining this stinking and terrible horror.

I'm not sure a horse will do that. – said the Serpent and smiled.

The little girl looked up at her quickly.

- And why do you doubt?

It's clear that horses don't poop on frogs in the stable. -

Mila the frog shook her head impatiently. It seems that this will be her future task. Uh!

- Of course! When frogs don't even live in a barn.

- Basically, when you bypass the fertilizer and horses, it's important that you find Spidey and convince him to come to the Fountain of Wishes in the evening – Merman Fasel explains to her as if it's something she does every day, running around the barn and dealing with spiders in the corners – preferably somewhere... at night...

- But why exactly – in the evening?

- Yes, how is he going to see what it says when it's dark? - asked Rinnie the toad.

Merman Fasel was more than enthusiastic about the new plan of liberation that was in front of them.

Dessy spends the whole day at the fountain. It might be a little strange to see frogs, a blue spider and a merman in one group that...

Frog Mila nodded her head and quickly interrupted him in this presentation.

- Okay, you assured me. I can do it!

Rinnie couldn't help but see it.

Water harmony is the most important thing.

- Exactly!

Mila the frog was already slowly working out the plan of work that was in front of her.

- I'm going to go there and tell Spidey to come to the Fountain. Then he will write a letter that the boring storks Tropp and Mexy will take to Rome, of course, straight into the hands of his fiancé, Gianni.

Rinnie couldn't help but say:

- Yes, since that poor Gianni didn't get a reply to a single letter to Dessy, and there were some... 1,2,3,4,5,6,7... letters. It is possible that now he will be fascinated when our letter arrives where we will tell him that ...

Merman Fasel sighed deeply.

- That Dessy fell unhappily in love with me ...

- But then we need to tell you exactly how you ended up there - said Rinnie the toad. Everything had to be put in the sun. There were no secrets now. If they keep silent about something, they may never reach that super peak of liberation that they have persistently strived for.

- I think it will be enough to say that it is enough to become a marman. And then let Dessy decide for herself who she wants for herself.

Rinnie the toad, who had already begun to tire of the conversation, just shrugged.

-Yes I do. That will be enough!

Frog Mila smiles happily.

- And too much!

- But how come Dessy didn't fall in love with you when you were an ordinary cat? - The snake couldn't help but ask this clever, thoughtful question.

- Because girls her age don't fall in love with cats, they fall in love with boys - Merman Fasel explained.

- And you're not a young man now, either - Rinnie remarked the toad, for she had seen many young workers on the farm and knew what they looked like.

- Yes, I didn't! – Merman Fasel shook his head.

The snake was strangely thoughtful and stared at his golden beautiful tail with which he was scurrying around.

- That's what makes this issue unusual.

7.

And of course, the very next morning they threw themselves into solving this arduous and exhausting task. It was impossible for a group from the fountain to reach such a distant destination as the stable. Logically, the fountain group never even dealt with these thoughts about the barn, or that they might be staying in the barn, even if only for a short time. It was a place that seemed unattractive, foreign, huge, had a strange and smelly smell and seemed like a place from which it would certainly never be very happy to return to the water.

Dessy was having breakfast at the time , which seemed fantastic for this small water crew. Mila the frog stepped out of the fountain very carefully , first checking tosee if the terrain was clean enough. That is, are those two voracious feathered monsters of the genus in their place? The storks Tropp and Mexy were there, beautifully nestled in their nest.

A white neighbor's cat, a true friend in the enormous trouble that befell them, was sitting on the edge of the fountain. She waited patiently for this little frog Mila to finally squirm over all those water lilies and reach the edge where the cat was staying. For a short time, the Merman Fasel also protruded from the water, as well as the fish Miklay and the toad Rinnie. The storks were still quietly swarming in their nest and didn't pay much attention to what was happening at the fountain.

Fish Miklay looked in front of him and noticed that Dessy was out of water.

- I thought that girl Dessy would never even go out to eat!

The white cat, who would have liked to eat him at another opportunity, now just looked patiently at his claws on his left paw.

- You can't have an empty stomach all your life, can you, Fasel? – the white neighbor cat looked at Fasel, whom she had known for a long time, but in that other four-legged and hairy form. – I think I liked you more as an orange rolled-up cat than like this ...

Merman Fasley just smiled.

- You don't know what's good, White cat.

Rinnie looked around and in the air. There was nothing suspicious. Just a couple of clouds out there somewhere very, very far away, but the clouds were never suspicious.

- Where's Tropp and Mexy?

They're up in the nest. "Rumble, as usual," replied the white cat, who had put his left paw on the concrete fence on which he was sitting.

- You, white cat, you have to protect me from their possible attacks! – said the frog Mila, of whom we must now say that she was really scared with this terrible scouting task. Now, a little frightened, she stared at the white cat for whom all this was not such a terrible undertaking.

- Of course - the white cat confirmed.

- But who can really guarantee that maybe you won't eat me either? - asked the frog Mila, because some cats still liked to catch frogs, and if they didn't eat them, then they would play a little acrobatic games with them.

The white cat was genuinely and gentlemanly astonished at this unusual "bon appetit" proposal.

- And what would I eat ordinary little frogs? You're not even cooked, but...

- Some cats catch lizards, so... – reminded her the frog Mila. That was a smart statement.

- I used to like lizards – Merman Fasel remembered his rare and beautiful delicacy.

- But not – frogs! So Frog Mila – are you going or not? I'm the neighbor's white cat and I can't sit there forever ... – she reminded her in a slightly impatient voice.

Mila the frog sighed deeply again. Her heart was beating very hard. She could have ended up in the beak of those horrible gluttons in an instant.

- You're right to know. It's time to embark on this crazy quest adventure for Spidey. I've never been on an adventure like this before.

Merman Fasel was already looking around him anxiously . Desssy could come at any moment, and then he would surely get another juicy kiss.

- A barn adventure?

- It's important that you escape the storks - Rinnie the toad explained, which she had said about thirty times by then.

- And to make sure that a horse doesn't poop on you. And that's all! – said Merman Fasel, who himself had fortunately escaped this terrible fate several times.

- Come on, dear! This is how we draw the attention of the storks, and Dessy, who is about to come back – said the White Cat.

-You're right! - confirmed the frog Mila bravely. - Let's go!

And she came out of the fountain, and the white cat followed her slowly. The team that stayed in the water watched after them for the next few moments.

- Do you think it will work? - asked Rinnie the toad.

- If it doesn't work, then Rinnie you will go!

Toad Rinnie was surprised by this proposal. It was as if it took her a few moments to compose herself.

- I? But why me?

Merman Fasel took a quick look at her.

- Because it would be strange for me to go to the barn now, and for the boss Demetrisio – by chance – to stumble upon a merman.

Then they concluded that enough of this outside conversation, because dessy threatened to return to the fountain again soon. Meanwhile, the white cat and the frog were slowly making their way across the grassy patch towards the stables where the riding horses were. The two storks, of course, must have noticed this strange and unusual phenomenon - a white cat and a small frog that jumped around its front legs.

- Tropp! - said Mexy.

- Say Mexy!

- Do you see anything unusual about the fountain? - asked Mexy, who closed her eyes a little, as if convincing herself that she was really seeing what she was seeing—a white cat and a little jumping frog.

Tropp, who was dreaming wonderfully just then, just quickly rubbed his eyes and avoided it.

- I see a neighbor's white cat, sometimes she wanders around this yard. In fact, since Fasel the cat left, she comes a little more often.

- I meant - that - in front of her? - said the stork Mexy, who then finds something as funny as little frog drumsticks.

I don't see anything good from here. Is there something in front of her?

- How blind you are. Well, that's some kind of frog.

It was only then that Tropp realized that there was actually a small frog in front of the white cat, which seemed to be protected by the white cat. A strange and unusual phenomenon in the yard.

- A frog and a cat?

- And they don't seem like a couple in love to me.. – said the stork Mexy, who really liked the theme of infatuation and sympathy. But she had never seen a Viennese cat and a frog in tandem.

- But that cat follows that frog that... That... Going to the barn with the horses. Now I see! Simply unbelievable! – only now did the stork Tropp get up and follow the events in the yard. Indeed, the white cat and the little frog were moving away towards the stables with the horses. But what will a frog in a stable do with horses?

- That's what I think too. That white neighbor's cat may have been a little sniffy. Who knows what the food is with? But come on, Tropp, get up for once. You've slept enough! It's time to see what kind of frogs this is all about!

And the two storks then fly towards the frog and the white neighbor cat.

Mila the frog, who had been jumping all the time on the grassy surface, which seemed to be continuous from her frog perspective, like a huge marathon without end, now looked away and noticed the two voracious storks flying towards them.

- Attention! Be careful, white cat. – warned her the frog Mila. – Bird artillery is on its way.

- On the way?

- I mean, now they are on the fly. Quick, quick! I've got to get to the barn as soon as possible. We will be safe there. Come on, quick, quick! I'm going to distract them...

And then the two storks flew over the new delicacy they wanted to fry. But Mila the frog successfully hid under the cat, feeling that those horrible cat hairs were covering her and sticking to her. He didn't count on this, on a hairy shelter. Yet the most important thing was to survive.

Then, in a somewhat ridiculous way and very slowly, they made their way towards that barn which was not so far away now. The two storks were still boring by default. They kept flying over the white cat, which made the whole situation really tedious.

- O-o-o-h! This is not going to be good.

The frog, who was terrified, patiently said the word:

- And what is it?

- Dessy's back to the fountain - remarked the White Cat, who knew that they had no chance of coming back in the next few hours.

- Oh, no! This means that we will be here in the company of horses until dinner. Look at how much their legs are ... tail ... – she said it in astonishment with fear, staring at the big, horse-like buttocks that were in front of her. It was indeed a pretty place, seen from a frog's perspective. But she wasn't here to give impressions of the interior and ambience.

- Imagine if they sat on top of me - sighed Mila the frog, aware that she didn't know what would have been worse for her then, " if one of the horses had tasted it as nicely as a pancake, or if Tropp or Mexy had fried it for a morning delicacy.

- You'll have a very good chance of being pooped by a horse.

During this time, the Merman Fasel and the Serpent and the Fish Miklay were swimming underwater. They look at Dessy who has appeared upstairs like something gloomy and terrible that obscures their view of the brighter side of life.

- Oh, no! Do I see it well? asked Miklay the fish.

- You see it right! Dessy went back to the fountain again," said the Snake.

- Then our frog Mila will not come back until the evening - Miklay the fish noticed.

-Maybe!

- Why do you say maybe? - asked Merman Fasel.

A horse is stepping on it or something. – said the Serpent.

Merman Fasel was disappointed with this possibility, which was clear and very dangerous.

-Uh! I don't think we'll ever get rid of these girls.

- It's a pity that you, Fasel, can't fall in love with her. It would be a wonderful romantic love at this stud farm. And the problem would be solved! The Serpent remarked, and that was an observation which it would have been better to keep to itself.

- I think Gianni from Rome is the only one who can help you with that at the moment.

Meanwhile, the two storks, Tropp and Mexy, were now staring at Dessy, who found herself in the same spot where she had stood staring at the water.

- Dessy is here again? - remarked Tropp.

- As far as I can see – it is!

- How strange! If I were her, I would visit museums, go to Venice or go to fashion shows, and she ... – said the stork Tropp. He's seen a lot of things in his life, but he's almost never seen anything like this.

- I've been in the water all day and I don't know what to expect. A prince on horseback... – Mexy remarked anxiously. – Princes don't jump out of the fountain. At least so far, they haven't!

But let's look at her. Better than some psychiatrist, maybe we finally understand what she is looking at so much in that horrible pond ...

And the two storks came back to their nest and were amused by Dessy who was just doing what she did every day, very nicely and very faithfully – she was looking at the water.

During this time, two brave and courageous fighters, a white neighbor cat and a frog named Mila, successfully arrived at their destination. So there was a real little circle of introductions between Mile the frog and Spidey and the horse.

- Please? – the blue spider Spidey ran into this little frog Mila, trying to understand the whole suggestion he had just heard but which he didn't understand well. It was as if the idea went in one ear and out the other.

- You heard it right – said the frog Mila and nodded her head at that.

- To go to Dessy's room and try to find the address of Gianni from Rome, and then ... – he was trying to understand the meaning of what he needed to do, what he was told was important for some level ... There is some harmony... Wait for what?

- Then you steal the paper and the pen to write him a love letter! - said Wicky the horse, slowly, as if it were something Spidey the blue spider does every morning for recreational purposes.

- You didn't get it right, Wicky. It's not a love letter. – said Mila the frog. Everything has to be said as it really is.

- Already? - asked the foal Jeanna, who was standing beside them, interested in all this talk and interesting suggestions for all sorts of scribbles that were necessary for someone there in Rome.

- About the warning! Gianni has to come here and do everything to make Dessy lose interest in Fasel. She's been standing there all day looking at the water! We used to have 3 of them, and now we have Dessy. That means we can't do music and opera during the day," Mila the frog quickly explained, concluding that she might sweat from so much strain .

- I understand, it's all because of the movement - said the foal Jeana.

- No. We are the best frog orchestra in the world and we sound much better underwater.

The foal Jeanna stared at her in surprise.

- I've never heard you underwater before!

- It's because horses don't swim underwater - Mila the frog explained to her this clear and eternal fact.

- That's not the point! - said Wicky the horse.

- It's all about water harmony... – sighed the frogand Mila. – The level is important!

- And about the fact that this Gianni , who I don't even know, should come here and solve the whole problem with Dessy and Fasel, with the frogs and the water calm.

- Exactly! - confirmed the frog Mila. - Everything is very much ruined again! We're just like scumbags.

Wicky nodded his head quickly.

- Frog scab! Maybe Fasel should become a cat again.

The little girl quickly shook her head.

- He doesn't want that! He does not like fleas!

Spidey the spider nodded quickly. He knew the spoiled cat Fasel well.

-That's true! I can confirm that! So, in my opinion, it remains for you to restore your watery, harmonious dignity.

- It's a few hours of fear to see that address, to steal a piece of paper and a pen, and then see you all at the Fountain in the evening.

The blue spider Spidey, however, was a bit conceited by this idea of real plaintiffs from Demetrisio's barn.

- I don't think that Gianni has ever received a letter from the spider from Demetrisio's barn.

- And I don't think Gianni has ever received any letter from this stud farm, so your barn scribble will surely be delighted - the frogguessed and Mila who almost felt sorry for that young boy. But now was no time for regrets.

- Good! - confirmed Spidey the spider , who knew that he would now have to go to Dessy's room, which seemed a little distant and unreachable from that angle in the barn. But with a little effort –

everything could be done today. – Someone needs to save the company in the Fountain, and it seems to be me again!

8.

And of course, the blue giant spider Spidey decided the very next day to do his task that was intended for him, which refers to several great endeavors: to find and remember Gianni's address, to steal a pen and a letter and paper. It seemed like something huge and impossible now, but it was certainly doable. Who else can do it better, if not him – the ideal little creature from the dusty barn.

So now, throwing his threads and moving at some standard speed for a spider, he walked towards Dessy's room. I've been here a long time ago, but there's nothing interesting about it . Just an ordinary room. There weren't even flies, which seemed really unbelievable and not at all spectacular, and he would peek his head out there again.

The room was still beautiful and decorated. The color of the walls was slightly different than last time, there was not a single fly – such an interesting and super interest. Basically, he was already bored, as soon as he poked his nose there. But now he wasn't here to interpret the color of the walls or everything else. It was filled with a floral scent that seemed strange to him, quite different from the smell of manure.

And very successfully throwing his threads around, he entered the room through the open window, quite happy that Dessy was in her standard and usual place, and that he was here all alone now.

- Woew! What a beautiful place this is here! – he said that and threw a thread long enough to reach a crystal, large, expensive chandelier over an armchair. He climbed up on the chandelier and looked down and around him for a short time.

It's a better view than in that room. So, it's up to me to find that letter where Gianni's address is written . It works so simply in my mind. Reading and reading flowers is not the same thing. I don't even know what color the letter is: white, pink, yellow, blue... So, here I am! On the mirror! And everything is so clean and everything smells nice ...

He looked around with sincere interest and then saw some papers on the closet. Just as he was about to go there, quite determinedly, the door of the room opened and the maid Merkez went inside

-Wow! Maid Merkez! But what kind of rags and brooms are they on that coffee table that she pushes inside? – asked Spidey the spider, who watched as the elderly maid gagged and pulled in a cart with accessories to clean the room. She pushed the cart inside, and he stared in amazement at the assortment of this not at all fun tool.

- Tidying up the room! - said the maid Merquez as if she were humming. - Twice a week continuously ...

Spidey flinched and got a little serious.

Tidying up the room? Ooo! I'm done! My nightmare has come true. I didn't want to end up like this. under the cloth.. What's going to happen to the water in the water? Fast! I have to get that letter quickly... I guess it was written by Gianni.. – and remembering his dream he had recently had, and the horror with those rainbow brooms, he now realized that he was really going to end up under some kind of melt or rag. A place he never imagined to end up.

And then the maid began to clean up the room. Of course he was careful not to let her notice him. He threw down the spider's thread and got hold of that beautiful place he saw, which was called the closet. Just when he got to the part where he saw some of Gianni's letters stacked, the maid Merquez was going to do her business right there.

- Life is beautiful! Life is so beautiful, and I'm with a rag – again she hummed happily to pass the time. She wasn't much of a singing talent, but Spidey wasn't a first-rate judging panel of judges either.

Just then, the blue spider Spidey escaped her rag, she didn't notice or touch it. He was hidden, breathing very hard. The nightmare was about to become real.

- I'm glad she's not in the corner now. I wonder what you'd think then?

And then he turned to a corner of the house that he had overlooked. He waited for her to go on with her business, and she quickly got to those letters and tried to remember the address that was indicated there. And then, without even knowing it, he tied a pen to himself, which seemed too heavy, and took it with one free leg, and there were several, and some paper. Then, again very skillfully avoiding the gaze of the hard-working maid, Merquez crept out of the room, aware that if he ever came to the stable again, he would go on a vacation where he would do nothing except rest from this arduous task.

And he slipped out of the room through the window , aware that the dream must have been like a warning, and that next time he would watch what he was dreaming.

A little weary when he was already in the tree, he felt that he was losing some of his strength, so he turned over into the bush. He was lying there and breathing heavily.

-I did it! I saw the address and I stayed alive!

He closed his eyes, aware that the barn was really too far away for him now, but that he would surely reach it in the course of the day

And that night, the group had a superb arrangement to gather around that fountain.

But nothing special was happening now, everyone was as if in anticipation.

- What's going on now ? - asked the toad Rinnie, who was sitting on the water lily, trying to make a nice and cultural splash.

Spidey stood on that horse and watched the territory. We had to make sure that the ground was clear. He stared at Dessyn, the persistent figure at that window, because even when it was night, and she was in her room and her nightgown, she was still standing at the window, looking longingly at the fountain. And so it was now.

- She's still at the window - said Spidey.

- And he's looking here? – asked the frog Mila, who jumped a little on the water lily so that she could see Dessy's persistent figure.

- Yes!

Mila, like a real scout, then turned around and peeked into the water towards the team that was persistently standing there.

- Dessy is still persistently at the window!

Miklay the fish nodded.

- Beans!

- Say Miklay!

- Do you think Dessy will finally go to sleep? Or will he be lurking all night to see if you might want to peek out? She seems to know that we want to send a letter to Gianni in Rome, so now she's keeping an eye on the whole "Fountain of Wishes" all the time! – Mikay the fish remarked calmly. It was a nice but very clever observation.

- I think the most important thing here is to know that patience is a virtue! - explained Merman Fasel. He knew what shooting was like a cat, especially when he was in front of the entrance to a mouse hole where he waited for hours for a delicious and nice bite.

And finally, to the general delight of everyone there, Dessy finally walked out of the window and turned off the light. Mila the frog peeked out of the water again.

- And?

- She's gone - said Rinni, and sighed.

- We'll wait a little longer - Spidey the spider explained. - Until midnight strikes on the cathedral. Maybe Dessy is lurking in the darkness of her room right now.

And a few minutes later, midnight struck a little later on the cathedral. Dessy was already sleeping peacefully in her crib. Spdiey the blue spider, who didn't like going out late at night, especially not to hang on to that horse, now just yawned and tried not to fall asleep. And all the others, except the frogs, were well asleep.

-Society! It's time to write a letter! – said Rinnie, who peeked under the water to inform the patient underwater crew.

- Hm! – replied the blue spider Spidey, who flinched and yawned. It wasn't time to sleep now. Now you should take advantage of the time of peace at the fountain, which during the day is not or never. - Wouldn't it be better to do it tomorrow? I'm about to fall asleep.

- No! – cut him off the frog Mila, who was again at the water lily. – Now you're going to do it!

- Come on! - said Rinnie, the toad, peeking under the water.

And Merman Fasel slowly floated to the surface of the water and breathed in the air after such a long time that this procedure was extremely unusual for him. The fish Miklay followed him and appeared on the surface realizing that it was night, the starry sky and that nothing on Earth is so fun at night, because everything is a bit dark.

The air is clean! It's like we're crazy about the air up there.

And the spider Spidey then went about his work, which was reduced to him. The truth is that he didn't know all the letters very well, and he wrote some letters upside down, but he still tried to compose a letter where he told Gianni that Dessy was now in love with the merman Fasel who lives in the Fountain of Desires. And that all Gianni has to do now is come on the night of the full moon, throw in the gold coin and become a marman. So Dessy could choose the one she loves more – Merman Fasel or him.

- Are you sure they're letters? – asked the frog Mila as she watched in amazement as Spidey devotedly and diligently scribbled on the paper.

- What do you mean? - asked Spidey.

- Well, people are bored. They changed the letter many times.

- Even though this is a scribble, Gianni in Rome will know what to do and ... And a little more ... And... Over!

When at last he had finished his great work of writing what resembled a message from the estate of the landlord Demtriso, he quickly mounted the horse, from where he stared attentively and angrily at the paper and his beautiful scribble.

- What are you doing up there, Spidey? - asked Miklay in surprise.

- Don't you see? - asked Spidey. - I'm reading my letter. I think everything is fine. There are a few grammatical errors ...

- Don't worry about grammar now, Spidey! - said Mila the Frog, quickly aware that with this letter they were halfway through the big job of getting rid of Dessy. No job has been easy, including this one.

- The letter is ready! - said Spidey the blue spider , very proud of his delightful way of scribbling. "Who's going to deliver it to those storks upstairs?"

'Well, the White Cat Next Door!' said the frog Mila, something that was almost taken for granted. Almost now, the frog Mila and the White Cat from the neighborhood have become real friends in this great and obligatory endeavor – removing Dessy from the fountain.

- Great, guys, now just to convince Tropp and Mexy to do it nicely... – the spider Spidey almost happy that he won't have to do it after all. Rode loved spiders, and he didn't want them on the menu tomorrow.

Merman Fasel, who lacked that tolerable level of water harmony, now just breathed a sigh of relief. The water harmony was almost there – a few steps away from him.

- I'm already relieved! Now all that remains is for that Gianni to come and solve the whole thing with Dessy.

I've come up with a few more details about all of this. It was a real, small, successful meeting that everyone was happy with. Now all he had to do was deliver that letter to Gianni in Rome and for him to come and sort out everything he thought needed to be solved very successfully and concretely regarding Dessy.

9.

And the next morning, the White Cat from the neighborhood got his new assignment. The letter given to her by Spidey the spider she quickly carried to the roof. There in the nest were the two idle storks, who were now staring in confusion at the white cat that had brought them the letter.

The two storks were even more confused when she explained to them nicely what they should do with the letter with an address on it, of course, if the pale Tropp and the confused Mexy might forget to whom and why they should hand over the letter in Rome. Rome is not a place in the neighborhood. And Gianni is not a name that rods remember so easily and beautifully ...

And when they had nicely clarified everything, to whom and why they were carrying that letter, both storks now felt much more important. I guess the most important thing in their lives was that they had to do that big task on the young man in Rome where they had been a couple of times, a place that is huge, where everything is teeming with people, and which is nice to visit sometimes when you really have to visit it.

Tropp, who had held the letter in his beak, now noticed that it was difficult to talk with the letter in his beak. But there is a first time for everything, and so there is a time with that task.

- Mexy!

- Say Tropp!

- Did someone tell you that it is very awkward to talk with a letter in your beak? - said Tropp, who was struggling to speak.

-I don't know. And I don't even want to find out... we should carry babies, not letters," Mexy quickly explained .

- Have we remembered that address, then? - asked Tropp, who had never been able to boast of great cleverness. It's not a priority for storks to be smart, is it?

- I think we are.

- Well, then let's go slowly... The sooner that Gianni from Rome comes here, the better for all those down there in that pond!' said Tropp, and the two storks then took off and set off on that long journey to Rome.

Their departure on the way to the Eternal City, was patiently followed by those two frogs - Milla the frog and Rinnie the toad. They sat in their standard positions – water lily leaves from where they could see everything that was happening on that roof.

- This is the first time in my life that I'm not so afraid of those storks right now! – said the frog Mila, who watched the storks slowly fly away from there and now become like two small dots somewhere far away in the sky.

- Me neither! But look, they take off and go to Rome ... I just don't know when they're going to get there? – said Rinnie the toad, who imagined that Rome as something that looked like that roof and maybe that left cave down there in the fountain.

- We have planned all this very well - sighs the frog Mila, almost proud of this endeavor, the super prosecutor from the stud farm of the owner Demetrisio.

- Yes, it's important to play as a team. Now all that remains is for Gianni to respond to our invitation and there you have it... Everything will be solved - croaks the toad Rinnie. It seemed so unified now that it was a real shame that they hadn't come up with something so exquisite and simple sooner.

- Yes, that would be wonderful.

And the two storks, Tropp and Mexy, only hoped that on the way to the eternal city of Rome there would be no rain or something like that. But luckily, the day was warm, beautiful and a real summer.

In the distance, they also saw the city where they had been a couple of times. Slowly they flew towards the place and all those houses, streets, trees, parks, buildings, churches, the Colosseum appeared to them. For a while, they flew over the Colosseum, always doing it without even knowing why.

- What a beautiful building, isn't it, Tropp? It's a little truncated on one side ... – she pointed with the wing of the Mexy stork towards the Colosseum, almost wondering when some construction workers will finish the work of this historic construction of the Colosseum. The building has always been abandoned and unfinished.

- This is the Colosseum. Roman emperors used to be there and they watched fights with lions - explained the stork Trop. He had heard it somewhere and remembered it, although it was not of great importance to him in the world of his bird's life.

- Ah, I understand! That is why there are so many statues of these cats in this Rome. Than...

- Mexy! - said Tropp.

- Say Tropp!

Tropp looked at the roofs of houses and the structures below him.

- I think it would be much better to focus on that address, and not to deal with Roman emperors and lions - it was a really smart suggestion. Now they are at work, not on a tourist tour of Rome.

- Okay, then tell me where to find that street ... – said Mexy, trying to remember how it sounded – Pomi ... Remember ... Drink...

- Rue Pompey! - said the stork Trop, who had taken great pains to remember the name of the street where the young man whose name he had forgotten lived.

- That's right - confirmed Mexy, who was looking down at the streets and rooftops of the houses here and there.

- Well ... Street ... at the moment ...

- I think I understand. There's something on every corner. As you can see, there is an inscription. Let's see what it's all about? – and they slowly landed on the corner where it said something that didn't resemble the name of the one Spidey the spider scribbled so that they would remember where they were going and for what reason.

And for a while, these two sturdy storks flew around some of the streets and read the signs. There was everything, and finally, after about two hours of dedicated and persistent work, which was a bit boring, they came to the sign they wanted to see.

- Hey Tropp, look... Via Pompeii.. Think we're in the right place? – said the stork Mexy ponsono, pointing to an inscription that resembled what the spider Spidey scribbled, only these letters were beautiful and upright.

- After... m... p ... e ... y ... – lamented the stork Tropp.

- Yes, I think we are. What's the point of Pompey?

- Maybe the name of a pre-Roman state or the name of a cat hunt or...

- Okay, well, we'll find out in time – confirms the genus Mexy, which didn't really reveal so many unimportant historical details.

But now it's not that important. The important thing is that we're here and we're going to find that number.

- Yes, let's go!

And the two storks then continued to do their job. By finding the house or apartment where Gianni was building, whom they then saw at that press conference and who was like everyone else - with his feet to the ground and his head on his shoulders. People are so similar.

And while these two devoted and hardworking storks were looking for this young man, Gianni was just then standing at that large patio window, looking out at the street in front of him. All his hopes for Dessy had died down, and now he wondered why that was so, and if it was worth worrying about Dessy being uninterested in him after all?

Prince Angust was visiting him again and gave him some good advice, but Gianni now thought that there was no point in putting any more money on romance or love if Dessy didn't appreciate it. It all came down to the marriage of convenience that was before him, which promised him, if nothing else, many good benefits.

- It's been 3,5 weeks and still not a word from my dear Dessy.

- She must have forgotten you - said Prince Angust. That now seemed safe and possible on the part of that impossible, obviously completely spoiled girl from that stud farm that was almost, well, the most famous horse stud farm in Italy.

- That's what I think too - he sighed deeply. Then he crossed his arms over his chest and went out into the terrace. "Perhaps I ought to forget her too, Prince Angust.

Prince Angust remained seated in that room and was now staring at him.

- Possible.

Then, by a truly spectacular coincidence , the two storks flew just above the building where Gianni lived and saw him standing on the terrace. It was like a real relief, because how could two storks even know in which apartment and in which room this Gianni was at the time? Spidey the Blue Spider wasn't so clear in his explanation...

The stork Mexy stopped excitedly in his flight and stared at the young man, almost in real disbelief.

- Tropp!

- Tell me, Mexy! - He'll show down. Tropp stops and looks.

- Yes, it's him! Well, you're a real genius, Mexy. In this huge city you manage to find Gianni. To me, the whole idea seemed abstract, like looking for a needle in a haystack.

- I'm going to be now. Now it's important for him to get out of that terrace and that you put the letter down – Mexy explained to him.

- Ha ha Mexy! Isn't that crazy? Usually storks say that we bring small babies, and now we deliver letters from those plaintiffs from that barn.

- There he is, he's gone away! - Mexy noticed that Gianni had gone inside from the terrace.

- Of course! As soon as he saw you and me, he decided to go inside.

And two storks then flew perm to that terrace. Now everything was much easier. All they have to do is hand over the letter to Gianni to decipher Spidey's hieroglyphs that he scribbled and everything will be solved. All the pain of the fountain group due to the lack of water harmony will be carried away by hand.

Meanwhile, Prince Angust and Gianni were still talking in the room.

- Your relationship was arranged by the boss Demetrisio. Maybe Dessy isn't even interested in love. Maybe you need to find a new love

And while Prince Angust was saying this, the stork Tropp descended all the way to that terrace. He flew very close and put down the letter so that both young men noticed it while he was carrying out his reconnaissance mission.

- Hey Gianni, what's that up there?

Prince Angust pointed with his hand to the paper that was falling to the ground and the storks that flew away from there to safe territory – into the air. Gianni, who was standing at those moments, saw this unusual event – the arrival and arrival of that stork postman. He walked over to the paper he had picked up and began to read the scribbles. Prince Angust, to whom all this was extremely unusual, approached Gianna. For a while, the two young men looked at the two storks as they watched them and then walked away from there.

- Storks brought us a letter?

Gianni was pensive as he looked at those birds that were now flying farther away.

-Rod? – he stared at the paper he held in his hands. – I think I've seen them somewhere, but I can't remember exactly where!

And the two storks who had successfully completed this task now turned back for a moment and saw that Gianni was holding the letter. Now they were able to return to the property. Everything that was happening now with Gianni, Dessy and Merman Fasel - was not in their care. Their work is now done.

They flew calmly on.

- Mexy, I think he took that letter!

- Obviously it is! The mission of handing over the letters from the prosecutors from the stud farm has succeeded and now we can all live in peace and idyll...

-Exactly! Now all that remains is for Gianny to reach the "Fountain of Desires" and for Fasel to find his water harmony again

And the two storks flew away from there.

At that time, Gianni and Prince Angust remained in that room. They looked at each other for the next few seconds as they stared at the letter that had been a little shabby as long as it had been in Tropp's stork's beak.

- The storks brought a letter? - he said it very carefully. He was thoughtful for the next few moments—as if he were thinking about whether storks should bring him a letter or a baby to the terrace. He unrolled the letter and began to read. Then he smiled, as if he had thought of something. – Of course, if I knew those storks. These are storks from the stud farm boss Demetrisio

Prof Angust was surprised by this new finding. Recognizing storks? This is not such a common case. He jumped a little

- Excellent! Dessy finally writes to you ...

Giani stared at those Spidey scribbles, seemingly surprised. As if he was expecting wonderful, beautiful, Dessy's love letters and romances, and not an inverted letter "a". He was a little disappointed that those storks had brought something from the stud farm that had little to do with Dessy herself.

This isn't Dessy, it's someone who barely knows how to write.

- Weird! And what does he say?

- Read!

He slowly handed him the letter, and for the next few minutes Prince Angust read what was scribbled there. He then very slowly put down the letter and looked at Gianni with a sincere question mark on his face.

- Now I understand why Dessy doesn't write to you. Now all the pieces are in place.

That's right, Angust. She fell in love with Merman Fasel, who lives in the "Fountain of Wishes" – he said it as if it were a common daily realization – that your fiancée is in love with some incomprehensible being in some pond over there.

- Merman? - asked Prince Angust, very surprised by this general and new fact from the stud farm. Aren't horses bred exclusively at the stud farm? – Aren't they mythical creatures?

- And while we were still putting up the statue of that horse Wicky, she seemed very disturbed and strange. She kept looking at the water ... So so? Merman? Beans? – he said that very thoughtfully. He once read the "Little Mermaid" by the writer Anderson. But no one there was really called – Fasel.

Prince Angust shrugged his shoulders quickly.

- It says that you should come on the night of the full moon and throw in one gold coin. The Water Spirit can turn you into a merman for two or three days, and Dessy can then make the right choice – you or that Merman Fasel.

Prince Angust stared at him for the next few moments. That was really interesting – to go to that fountain, throw in a zlantik and become a new memran. An interesting observation. It's as if it's something you do along the way – while going to the market or getting bread.

- What are you going to do, Gianni? - his friend looked at him with sincere interest in his eyes.

Gianni asked, somewhat surprised. As if there was anything to ask at all. – Well, I'll go to that "Fountain of Wishes". If that's the only way to know if Dessy really loves me – then I'm going to become some kind of mythical marman for three days.

And while he was saying this, we have to say that Gianni was very, very thoughtful.

And during that time – two storks real Roman postmen – Tropp and Mexy returned to the stud farm of the landlord Demetrisio. Straight to that group who were eagerly waiting to find out what the news was from that distant and mythical Rome, whether Gianni had received the letter, what he had said, and whether he had said anything at all.

At that time, luckily for all of them, Dessy was not present, and at the fountain there were – Merman Fasel, White Neighbor Cat, two frogs, Spidey and Miklay the fish who was just peeking out a little bit because he didn't like to be outside and breathe that air for a long time.Nothing without the good old smell of stale water and algae. Unbeatable.

The success of the mission is obvious. Good for you, Tropp. Bravo Mexy! – said Miklay the fish, delighted that the success of the mission was ensured with the commitment of all of them on equal terms. If something should be done right, it should be done in a group.

- We are so proud of ourselves - croaks the toad Rinnie.

- We found Gianni's address - said Mexy the stork, proud that they had succeeded in such an unusual plan that would otherwise never have occurred to them on any other occasion.

- Now all Gianni has to do is come and talk to Dessy - said Fasel thoughtfully. A beautiful, watery hamronia in all possible levels, was almost within their reach.

- Fasel, are you 100 percent sure you're not in love with her? - asked the blue spider Spidey, who was looking at him with a big question mark in his eyes.

-Yes I do. Can't you fall in love with her in the future? Near-distant-middle future? Bela, the neighbor's cat, asked him. Still, everything was possible today. Love comes slowly and suddenly, doesn't it?

- I honestly don't think so! I want to enjoy my water harmony, to hang around nicely and sing ... – explained Merman Fasel. There's nothing like singing and singing. Not even a hundred new underwater caves with crystalline stones can properly replace this.

- Okay, good! – nodded the Tropp stork.

- Just don't change your mind later! – Mexy the stork warned him.

Tropp nodded her head in those moments.

- Yes, Fasel! If you fall in love with Dessy, then it will be too late for everything.

- Well, I don't think I can fall in love with her! What could make me change my mind? - asked Merman Fasel very carefully. He was very thoughtful. He just shrugged, looking confused by the question.

10.

And during one of the following evenings, when the sun had already set and the moon was shining with all its splendor once high among the tiny, small stars, a taxi carriage was going to the stable of the owner Demetrisio. As it was very late, and Gianni did not want to appear with his loud car somewhere nearby so that all the geese, ducks, horses and dogs would not wake up, he decided to come close to the property with some carriage. The carriage was standing at the entrance of the station, and now he was riding very slowly and calmly, while he thought of that letter.

First of all, Gianni couldn't guess who had written that letter with the letter "a" twisted and with so many grammatical errors, but the meaning of it all was very clear. Now this young man was thinking of Dessy. To the wonderful beautiful and lovely Dessy who was sympathetic to him at first glance, but who will never seem to fall in love with him.

And why?

Because of some ordinary merman from that fountain or pond. The very realization that he, as a handsome and respectable young man of Rome, should jump into such a toadstool seemed unbelievable to him. But still, it might be worth taking the advice of the person who wrote that letter. Awaken that Blue old ghost and become the new merman in the "Fountain of Desires". That was the best decision. He's never been a merman, he's never wanted to be a merman, but anything can be achieved today.

Although everything was unbelievable to him, he now only occasionally looked out the window at the dark night illuminated by the full moon and at everything around him that was just surveilling himself.

- Are we close to the property? - He addressed the coachman in front of him very nicely and kindly.

- Just a little longer, Monsieur Gianni - said the old coachman, smiling.

- You're going to leave me about a mile away from Demetrisio's estate.

The coachman was surprised by these words. He couldn't help but ask.

- Aren't you going to visit your fiancée Dessy? – of course the older man knew that Dessy was his fiancée, it was a well-known and public matter.

- Well, I'm going, but... I want it to be a surprise!

The coachman nodded .

- I see!

A little later, the carriage slowly stopped, and Gianni got out of that carriage.

- You can go back to Rome now!

- And you, Mr. Gianni?

- I will stay as a guest for three days. And don't tell anyone I came here, okay? – he said it to him like a silent but very clear warning.

- As you say, Mr. Gianni.

And the carriage slowly went on. A few more moments later, there was a short neighing of a horse and the sound of a wheel turning on a gravel road. And Gianni slowly crept up to Demetrisio's stud farm. The stud farm was now plunged into complete sleep. The full moon was shining on everything in front of him, and now he could see very clearly the big house in the distance, the stables, the trees. Only one window had light, it was from Dessy's room. And when he came near, he saw the lawn, as well as the statue of Wicky the horse, and the fountain. There was a short croaking of frogs, but he paid no attention to it. He looked towards the house through all the windows. Everything was now in the dark, everyone seemed to be sleeping peacefully, and they had no idea that he was now here on this new and strange mission that had befallen him. However, he jumped over that wall very carefully and went inside the yard. He looked around very carefully and carefully.

- Now the only thing that matters is that no one notices me - he said quietly and more to himself, like a vague warning.

He slowly came closer to the fountain, from where he could see Dessy who jr was at the window. Gianni quickly and skillfully hid behind the bushes. She didn't even notice him, all the while she was looking at the fountain that was now clearly visible under the moonlight.

- So, it's true. There is really something in that fountain

He stared at her for a few moments, completely intrigued by the whole situation. He could never have thought that moments like this would come.

- All I need to do is put the gold coin in the water and make a good wish, I can't wait to see that Water Spirit too.

Dessy then slowly walked out of the window. She turned off the light to finally go to sleep.

Her fiancé, Gianni, waited a few moments to get to the fountain. Finally, he slowly sneaked towards the fountain. It was a very careful sneaking. He just hoped that no one would notice him.

He walked over to the fountain and threw a gold coin into the water. He didn't want to wait a minute. And he was interested, but it is really true based on what it says in this letter that this is a magical fountain of wishes.

The gold coin slowly fell to the ground. And it all happened again. As soon as the gold coin touched the ground, a blue powder was formed. The old Blue Ghost woke up again and started to scratch the surface of the water.

For the next few moments, Gianni and the Blue Ghost looked at each other silently. Gianni was completely surprised when he saw him, so he could not hide the expression of delight on his face.

- So, it's true! You really exist!

'Oh yes!' laughed the Blue Ghost, staring at the young man who had been looking at him so curiously. 'For very, very many decades and centuries, my boy... And you are?

- My name is Gianni. I come from Rome.

- Well, Gianni of Rome – what could the Blue Water Spirit of the Fountain of Wishes" do for you? - asked the latter, adjusting his black top hat that he always wore, even when he had slept peacefully for a century.

- My fiancée , Dessy , lives here, her father owns this stud farm and...

- But he's not the owner of me; I've existed here before him. Admittedly, I mostly sleep and rarely do I ever get woken up – the Blue Ghost replied.

Gianni looked at him for a few moments , and then smiled.

That's because they don't even know about you. And that's not what it's about! Dessy lives here, she's my fiancée and she's in love with Merman Fasel who resides here in this fountain. Admittedly, I've never had the opportunity to see him before! – this young man tried to quickly explain.

And what am I supposed to do now? Should I make Dessy fall in love with you?" asked the Blue Ghost.

- No! I'll be fair!

- It's nice to be fair!

- I'm going to be fair!

- It's nice to be fair. – confirmed the Blue Spirit.

- I want to become a merman for three days, so that she can decide who she loves better – Fasel or me! - said Gianni slowly.

The blue ghost stared at him for a few moments. He put his index finger to his forehead, as if he had a deep thought about it.

- Wait a minute, let me think about it! – for a while the Blue Ghost was thoughtful, and then quickly said. – All right! I'm going to make you a mermaid.

-Temporarily! It's been 3 days!

- Since lately, in a short period of time, several of them have come forward with the desire to be – mermans – this time I'll make at least one difference ... – said the Blue Ghost, who started to get a little bored with this serial merman making – as if young people today don't have any other interesting desires.

Gianni seemed thoughtful; he was a little suspicious.

- I'm going to make you a merman so that Dessy can make the final choice. You have a deadline of three days. In three nights, at midnight, this magic expires... If she chooses you and not Merman Fasel, you will return to the figure of an ordinary man and live happily and contentedly for the rest of your life.

Gianni nodded his head calmly. The young man was almost convinced of such an outcome.

- Yes, that would be nice!

- Indeed, it would be!

Gianni , however, couldn't help but ask.

- And what if she chooses Merman Fasel? – he was thoughtful.
And that can happen... Women's decisions are truly unpredictable.
But then what's going to happen?
The blue water spirit looked at him for a few moments.

- In that case, you will return to the form of a man, but you will not be here. You're about to wake up in your room. You'll forget you've ever known Dessy and Boss Demetrisio! You'll forget that you've ever been here, that you've seen me, that you've been a marman. You will simply have complete amnesia.

He shrugged his shoulders, as if for a moment he'd been hesitant about the whole idea.

It seems fair to me! So?

- All right! - replied Gianni, quickly after that, as if from a cannon. Turn me into a merman...

And immediately after that, the Blue Ghost made that blue smoke around him. Gianni stared in the air for a few moments. His clothes were gone, and in a second his legs were turned into a blue ponytail. And then suddenly Gianni, like a beautiful marman, found himself in the water of the old "Fountain of Wishes". He was surprised and looked around, and the Water Spirit disappeared and retreated again to the bottom of the fountain to resume his centuries-old peaceful sleep.

The snake was the first to notice that the new coin marman was found in the fountain.

- We've got a new merman again.

The fish Miklay stood beside him and looked at Gianni, who was looking around him with joy and curiosity.

-Yes... It looks like it's already being factory-made.

The snake immediately looked around.

- Where's Fasel?

- He's looking around the caves with Mila the frog! – Miklay the fish quickly replied, looking at the merman in front of him.

- I'm sure he'll be surprised to see that this Gianni has become a merman!- said the Serpent, aware that the endeavor of the accusers from the fountain had nevertheless borne fruit. Merman Gianni was here. Now it was all up to Dessy's final decision, which might one day be a wonderful, sunny day.

-Yes I do. But Gianni is different ...

- It has a light-blue tail!

The fish Miklay carefully measured the appearance of the merman that was in front of them, but to whom they were uninteresting. Gianni looked at the algae and aquatic colorful herbs that slowly swayed in their rhythm.

- And a necklace!

- You have a good observation. But look, now he swims and looks at everything around him ...

Miklay the fish was just curious.

-Yes. Snake, let's see what he's going to do now.

Both the Serpent and the Miklay Fish swam slowly after Gianni, keeping an adequate distance. Meanwhile, none other than Rinnie the toad slowly swam up to Gianni. She looked at him with sincere interest, especially his blue tail.

- Oh, you're a brand new money-changer! – Rinnie the toad noticed.

He turned slowly towards her and stared at the curious frog. He was surprised when he saw her.

- Oh well, that's some talking frog ...

Rinnie nodded quickly, almost proud of that fact.

- Yes, it is! My name is Rinnie.

- Rinnie, I'm Gianni - he introduced himself, very cheerful, because he never dreamed of what it would be like to be here under water

Rinnie tried her best to act as the true host of that fountain.

- I see you've received my letter.

Gianni was surprised when he heard what she said.

- Is that what you wrote?

Rinnie nodded her head again. I've been writing a letter two or three years ago.

-Exactly. In fact, Spidey the spider.

- Spidey? I didn't know spiders could write.

- He's not much of an expert on spelling!

Gianni remembered those scribbles and the twisted letter "a".

- That's what I noticed.

- He's not an expert in grammar either!

Gianni couldn't help but smile.

- And I noticed that!

- But anyway, now you're here with us! – croaked the toad Rinnie.

- Yes, and I didn't even know that the world underwater was so beautiful ... That fountain upstairs ... From the outside, it looks a bit shabby and old, but...

-Possible!

Gianni couldn't help but be completely honest.

Even the statue of Wicky the horse didn't improve the overall impression.

-Possible!

Gianni stared at this strange, colorful, aquatic animal in amazement.

- You keep saying the possible!

- Because I'm an impossible frog!

Where's the mermaid?

- Beans?

- Well... - Gianni thought to himself, although he couldn't imagine the other merman. I don't know anyone with that name...

I didn't even know he could be called that. So far, it's called Faseln.

Gianni smiled. Both he and Rinnie the toad then slowly swam on.

- Fasel! Chatterbox! Crazy name!

Rinnie smiled briefly.

- That's what I'm saying, a lot of people have such crazy names.

Meanwhile, the fish Miklay and the Serpent swam after them quite curiously and calmly, keeping a safe distance.

- It seems to me that Rinnie the toad and the merman have become friends! – remarked the Snake, who was measuring the two in front of her.

- It looks like they are... She always makes friends with everyone, regardless of the type of ...

- He may find out some of Gianni's weak points, but I doubt he'll tell us.

- Probably not!

They then swam a little slower, so that the merman Gianni and the toad Rinnie moved away from them. However, then the Merman Fasel and the frog Mila slowly swam to the fish Miklay and Snake . They looked at the new merman and Rinnie with sincere interest.

Of course, Merman Fasel was delighted to finally see Dessy's fiancé from Rome in that fountain. It wasn't exactly something he wanted to see when he asked the Blue Spirit to be an ordinary marman, but life brings all sorts of new experiences and outbursts. Now he felt a sincere satisfaction in finally getting rid of Dessy's constant presence,

- Oh, well! - said Merman Fasel. - It seems to me that we have a new company.

Miklay the fish quickly nodded.

- Obviously yes!

The snake was still standing upright and upright, although it was not her favorite position in the water.

- Merman Gianni decided to join us. The "Fountain of Wishes" is richer for another new merman.

- I'm glad he didn't want to be a shark. Then you certainly wouldn't be able to beat him, Fasel! – remarked Mikay the fish, who didn't even know what those sharks looked like, but he compared them to those three dangerous catfish that lived here before – gorgeous, fat and gluttonous.

- Do you think we should fight here? No one was fighting here, except Wicky and those catfish.. – noted Merman Fasel. That observation was correct.

- It just seems logical to me that two male specimens are fighting for Dessy's affection - said Miklay the fish.

- Men on land must sometimes fight for the affection and love of a woman ... – sighed the Snake.

- It is safe and possible. Maybe they are waging some wars, going on attacks, killing... I think the people up there are a little crazy... – Miklay the fish remarked, all happy that he was just an ordinary colorful fish in that fountain and that he was spared the human understanding of love.

- When I was a cat I didn't notice any fights on the property. Only the singers were fighting, and sometimes, but even that wasn't exciting! Feathers flew a little ... – Merman Fasel could not help but recall some interesting unwoven feathered fights.

- There you go! And the singers are fighting for the favor of the hens ...

- I'm sure we'll have to take a look at it, but I'm going to have to give up on it right now. It would be okay if I gave him Dessy's love and heart – said Merman Fasel with a note of sincere hope and relief. He nodded his head slowly as he said that. Then they were finally noticed by the merman Gianni. He quickly turned to Rinnie the toad, who, like a true host in the fountain, still felt all the notes of sincere pride in being exactly what she was.

- Is that the Merman Fasel? - asked the Merman Gianni, as he jealously and questioningly measured his rival. He looked at his golden face, his posture... It's unbelievable that Dessy had something like this in her garden. No wonder she never replied to a single letter, justifying herself with love for horses. She didn't just say that the horse was very beautiful, that he had a fish tail and that he lived in her fountain!

- Is. It has an orange-gold tail.

- It seems average to me - said the merman to Gianni jealously. "I don't understand what Dessy saw in it. But come on, let's go.. I'm really jealous of this guy and I'm ready to do a lot of bad things to him – to rip off his head, arms, legs... Tail

And they came quickly and swiftly to the merman of Fasel and all those who were around him. Of course, Merman Gianni seemed quite angry and haughty at this moment.

- Well, we're going to meet Merman Fasel!- said Merman Gianni very proudly.

- It seems so - replied Merman Fasel, a little surprised by the fury of Dessy's fiancé.

- So you're that disgusting bastard who stole my fiancée Dessy's heart? - he asked very angrily. Merman Gianni then quickly approached him and got in his face. The situation was very tense in those moments of this first skirmish. Everyone was looking at them excitedly. But Merman Fasel very tactically slowly stepped back a little further.

- I didn't do that on purpose! - said Merman Fasel, and that was the real truth.

- But you've done it!

Toad Rinnie couldn't help but say:

- It's not for me to interfere, but does that Dessy love you, Mr. Gianni?

Merman Gianni looked angrily at this toad. I had such beautiful and different plans about three weeks ago with Dessy. And not to be in this pond with a bunch of amphibians ...

- No one ever asked her if she loved me! - said the merman angrily to Gianni.

Everyone looked at him in amazement.

- What do you mean – no one asks her? - asked Merman Fasel cautiously.

- Well, no! - replied the merman to Gianna.

- Very strange - said Miklay, the fish, who couldn't understand why the Merman Gianni was acting so repulsively.

- That's what I think too! – croaked the frog Mila.

Her father arranged for us to get engaged. No one has asked Dessy anything, and no one will ever ask her anything! – said the merman Gianni, aware that the word of the master of Demetrisi was now the last word that would certainly have to be listened to.

Merman Fasel was surprised.

- What matters is how she feels.

Merman Gianni waved his hand carelessly.

That's not important at all! It's important to get married as soon as possible. I will inherit some property, and her father will provide me with top business opportunities in the bank and oil stocks. It's car time, the carriage season is over, but you haven't figured it out yet. I'm going to get richer, I'm going to get rich, I'm going to be able to get a lot of things. It doesn't matter what Dessy feels.

A little girl who didn't really understand love and sympathy couldn't help but notice:

- That's a bit cruel!

Fish Miklay was stunned.

- That's what I think too!

- And the Serpent was still standing upright.

- It's not fair to Dessy.

- A lot of things in life aren't fair. Here, for example, you merman Fasel! You're a big problem for everyone right now. You have created problems for me and spoiled some plans with your presence here! – said the merman to Gianna, who turned around a little and pointed to her with his hands. – In this water. It is true that the aquatic atmosphere is truly colorful and top-notch, you spoiled many of my plans up there on the surface.

Merman Fasel was now slowly beginning to get angry with this impossible and haughty fiancé of Dessy. He didn't know why the girl didn't answer his letters.

- Gianni, I had no intention of ruining anyone's plans. And on top of that, Dessy's eternal presence spoiled my water harmony that I wanted to have here!

- Because she saw you and fell in love with you - Gianni told him about this indisputable and clear fact. He was angrily measuring Merman Fasel, he couldn't help but guess. "Even though you look completely average, blue eyes and slicked-back black hair. Only that golden tail gives you grades higher than average, but ...

- Well, Dessy didn't ask me what I wanted and wanted – she just imposed herself here!

Merman Gianni smiled contemptuously.

- Well, Fasel, you didn't even ask what Dessy was thinking and how she was feeling. And surely, since she's stupid and because she's a woman, she feels very bad as she stands by that fountain for hours, waiting for you to peek out and follow your tail a little on the water!

Merman Fasel remembered, briefly, that first meeting and Dessy's sudden kiss.

-Yes I do. You're right. I've never wondered about her feelings and thoughts. I don't even know what she thinks.

Why does it matter if she loves me or what she thinks? Because you see—he weighed them all at once —None of you care what Dessy thinks, and it doesn't matter to me now. I'm not sure about the problem and the meaning of this conversation.

- I think all of this is cruel to Dessy - remarked Mila the frog, who didn't know whether to start pitying that rich daddy's daughter.

- I'm a frog, and I think so too! – croaked Rinnie the toad.

Life is cruel. She's a woman and she'll get used to it somehow. In life, it is important that a woman has a rich husband, that she can live well, and that love slowly disappears over time! – the Merman Gianni muttered contemptuously, and in those moments he was looking at his great rival, which was the Merman Fasel. As if he had come up with something interesting, he said quickly. "But, here, this is how we'll work!" We'll let Dessy make a nice choice in the next three days. First – maybe me, who can afford a lot for her and who plans to advance in my career. Or else – and that's you Fasel – he said it all with a note of ugly and clear mockery. – You are an ordinary marman from the "Fountain of Desires" who has neither property, nor wealth, nor the possibility of career advancement. You're almost on the level of a homely, watery, unusual, tailed pet with no future or anything. I think she might be better off loving a tramp, and I'm almost certain that Boss Demetrisio would never approve of your relationship. He's a successful and powerful man, and you're a fasel... You're an ordinary amphibian, without a puppy and a kitten and anything!

Merman Gianni seemed to be sure of everything he was saying, now a little more relaxed and freer he swam a little further, and then quickly and deftly came back.

- I don't even know why I should fight for her favor with you, when the matter is already perfectly clear from the beginning!

Finally Merman Fasel spoke up after all these terrible words. It must be said that Merman Fasel was now in real disbelief and just shook his head.

-Amazing! You don't love her or appreciate her at all.

Merman Gianni laughed sweetly and with a gruff voice .

- Ha ha ha ha! And who says that? You, Fasel?! Well, you don't like her either... You don't care about her feelings or affection.

Merman Fasel stared at him in complete disbelief.

- You're her fiancé.

Rinnie the toad, like Miklay the fish, had just been completely stunned.

- And maybe the future husband!

- So what then? - He shrugged his beautiful shoulders to the merman Gianni and put on his beautiful blue necklace that he wore around his neck.

What kind of life will she live next to you? She's going to die of sadness and emptiness – remarked Merman Fasel, who now began to feel sorry for Dessy's future, horrible life.

- He will get used to it. What kind of life is she living here right now, waiting like crazy for you to peek in and squirt your tail right now? I think Fasel, you're the last in this world right now that can point the finger at someone, and at least you have the right to criticize me. I think I've said what I mean, and now I'm going to go see some of those caves. I'm going to be here for 3 days, so I'd like to get to know the whole community. When I beat you and marry Dessy, I'm sure I'll never have the opportunity to be here again and to be a merman – as the merman Gianni was aware that in those moments he had said everything he thought it was necessary to say, now he calmly and carelessly waved his hand. This is the first time he's ever been here.

Everyone looked at him in amazement and with some horror . They were quite worried.

- Do you have the impression that Dessy's life is not written well if she lives with this Gianni? - asked the frog Mila.

I'm sure there's going to be a waterfall on her.

Merman Fasel was now really thoughtful about everything he had realized in the last ten minutes.

- That's what I'm thinking too, Ryan. I'm so sorry to hear that you even invited this guy here.

Fish Miklay looks at him with pity.

Oh my gosh, the train has passed.

Merman Fasel was now very thoughtful because of Dessy. But he knew that he would leave some of his current thoughts for himself and for tomorrow.

That morning, Merman Fasel thought of Dessy.

It was the first time he didn't think of her as Dessy, his former mistress, or as Dessy, the intrusive and persistent creature who hangs on that fountain all day long, wanting to see him.

He thought of her as the girl who was in love with him. And in those moments, some beautiful feelings begin to arise in him, which until yesterday morning he did not even think could arise. He remembered Dessy's kiss she had given him, her insistent presence, the songs she sang as she touched the surface of the water with her hands. And now he could lose it all , and that was because he was the one who had asked for this horrible man to be summoned here by her fiancé from Rome.

Fasel thought that he had never known anything more disgusting than him. I'm so excited about Dessy and her future. Demetrisio didn't even know Gianni when he decided to marry Dessy. And what can he do now, as an ordinary merman Fasel?

Merman Fasel had the vague impression that he was in a terrible position. He wanted to help Dessy, and yet on the other hand it seemed utterly impossible for him to do anything about it. He was just an ordinary marman in that fountain, and maybe Gianni was right. He had nothing to offer that beautiful girl. Demetrius would never accept it.

I accepted – like what? – I asked myself. He was just an ordinary marman, after all, and it was his job to enjoy all levels of water harmony, and only occasionally to come to the surface, and then, when no one saw him, he slings his tail on the surface of the water with sincere pleasure. It was all so ordinary, impersonal, boring. Now it seemed to him that it would be better to occasionally come to the surface of that water and get closer to Dessy.

But now the train has passed! – he thought to himself, and almost wondered why he had come up with such a terrible idea of inviting Merman Gianni here. Until yesterday he was so happy, he had Dessy all to himself without even realizing it.

And so, in those thoughts that swarmed in his head and changed his feelings for Dessy, he was also found by the fish Miklay. At first, Miklay the fish looked at him in amazement, so worried and lost in thought, and then at last he decided to approach him and find out what it was that was now tormenting the beautiful golden-tailed merman.

- Are you very worried, Fasel? - said Miklay the Fish.

Merman Fasel, who had been lost in thought, now flinched when he noticed that he was no longer quite alone.

- I thought about something - replied Hey Merman Fasle.

Miklay the fish swims all the way up to him.

- And our new coin merman is now examining water caves, do you know that?

Merman Fasel, who was now thinking of Dessy with a lot of tenderness, just waved his hand.

- No. It doesn't even matter to me.

- How does it not matter to you? - asked the fish Miklay in amazement , who was looking at him inquiringly. What is so strange about the Merman Fasel today?

- I'm thinking about Dessy.

- Are you thinking about Dessy? – fish Miklay was very surprised by this statement. – Until a day or two ago you waited to get rid of her! You said that it violated your standard level of water harmony. She tried to kiss you, touch you, touch you. If someone told her that all she had to do was insert a gold coin and turn the Water Spirit into a mermaid, she would certainly do it. Then you two could live here like mermaids and do it happily ever after... If only you might be in love with her, like you're not...

- But maybe I could fall in love with her – Merman Fasel still decided to share some of his morning thoughts and observations.

It must be said that the fish Miklay was really amazed when he heard this.

-What?

Merman Fasel decided to be completely honest right away.

- I was thinking about her ... I think I can fall in love with her... In fact, since Gianni has been here and since he said what he said, I started to think differently about her!

- There you have it! I knew it might be like that – sighed Miklay the fish. Ah, how strange these people and mermans are . That wasn't the case in the fish world . It's lucky that I'm not a merman or a man – thought the fish Miklay.

- And how could you know that?

- Because you didn't have any rival here ... It's all about that! Logical! Now that you see that you have a rival, you have started to look at Dessy from a different angle. Isn't it a little late for that now? – Mikaly the fish noticed. It was exactly what Merman Fasel had been thinking about so persistently.

- I admit that I regret that we invited Merman Gianni. I think it would have been better if Spidey hadn't written that letter.

Miklay the fish nodded his head persistently.

Tropp and Mexy didn't even take him to Rome.

- Exactly . Better if they got the address wrong, than Gianni...

Miklay the fish seemed to be losing his temper a bit, so he decided to interrupt him.

- It's too late for any talk about it now!

- I agree with that.

- Now it's all up to Dessy's final decision! - said the fish Mikaly, aware that everything now, even Fasel's newfound infatuation, depends only on the decision of that girl up there.

- I agree with that.

Fish Miklay still saw in everything and some nice positive things.

And you may find a satisfactory level of your water harmony again.

Merman Fasel nodded his head. Yesterday was the most important thing in my life, but now...

- And I agree with that. And now I don't care so much about Ribo-Miklay. I'd like to go back in time to a few days ago. I wasn't even aware of how lucky I was. Can time go back a bit?

Miklay the fish shook her head in pity.

- No, Fasel. Now in the next three days we will see how everything unfolds.

- It's a pity that I'm not an ordinary cat right now, that I have my intuitive sense again.

Miklay, the fish, looked at him in amazement.

- Don't marmans have intuition?

- No! Maybe a little.

- Then you have to fight with Gianni and wait for Dessy's final decision - said Miklay. That was the only future for them , which they obviously built together.

- It annoys me that I imposed this problem on myself.

Fish Miklay just sighed. Now it was not worth crying for last year's snow. He fell, melted.

- It looks like you did! Next time, be a little smarter.

11.

And that morning was just like any other beautiful summer morning at the estate of the owner of Demetrisius. First, some animals woke up, then around five or six o'clock some workers began to do their usual daily work.

Dessy slept peacefully in her bed. Then the young girl began to wake up slowly. She heard the creaking of the cart in the hallway and knew that it must be the maid Merkez and that she was pushing the wheeled cart. She didn't think about the maid Merkez now. Nothing so ordinary and everyday could disturb her and wake her up from a beautiful daydream.

Dessy slowly stood up and put on a red dress with black puffs. She put a pink ribbon in her hair and was happy with her reflection in the mirror. Everything seemed so much more interesting and better since Merman Fasel had been here, and since she'd known he was here. That day, however, she thought about how she hadn't seen him for a long time . She knew that he was underwater, that he was watching her, that he was just the wonderful magical creature she had in her life. And that knowledge was not enough for her today . It was as if she wanted to have something much more than that, but there was no one with whom she could share her own thoughts, aspirations and observations. By the way, she had already given up on the idea of writing letters to some of her friends and telling them about that marman.

No one would understand her very well.

Now she slowly walked out into the warm morning air. She quickly greeted the maid Merkez and her father, and then walked on, followed by their persistent gaze.

- Maybe I'll see him again today, - she said to herself, as if with some hope. – Maybe, the day is long.

Merkez, the maid, who had been doing her standard morning activities, now looked at the young girl and shook her head.

- He goes to the fountain again.

- I don't understand what my daughter has been doing there for so long? - asked the boss Demetrisio as if in disbelief.

- I don't understand that either - said the maid Merkez

- But I think we should follow her and be on our guard from time to time! – replied the boss Demetriso, who watched as Dessy came to the fountain again and calmly watched the water.

For the next few moments, nothing special was heard, only the standard sounds that were usually heard on the property. A few bees were spinning around a lotus, and a pair of small frogs were sitting on the edge of the fountain watching the girl.

- Come on, come on, beautiful marman! It finally appeared – and slowly, with her right hand, the young girl Dessy touched the surface of the water.

Down at the bottom of the fountain she was calmly watched by the mermans: Fasel and Gianni, the fish-Miklay, then the two frogs: Rinnie and Mila, and there was the eternally equally stiff Serpent.

Merman Gianni noticed his fiancée appearing at the edge of the fountain. He saw her hand touching the water. And all this about her was now starting to really annoy him. Then he stood up and seemed extremely haughty. A little angrily, he turned his gaze towards Merman Fasel, whom he blamed for all that had happened.

- There she is my beautiful fiancée. Do you see, Fasel?

- How do you think she'll be surprised when she sees me there? I'm sure I'm the last person in this world at the moment who can be imagined, and as a mythical creature – a merman – in his well, or in a fountain. And it is she who looks into the water for a long time and waits. How funny is that, isn't it? I've been waiting for those letters too! – he said it as if he couldn't believe the reality he found here.

- And what's so funny about that? – Fasel flinched and stared at this disgusting Merman Gianni.

- You don't like her at all, and she seems to be burning with the desire to see you. So look at her! In fact, Fasel, don't even look at her. I don't think it makes sense for that! Soon Dessy will be mine alone, and you won't matter to anyone anymore! - he was extremely pleased with what he said, and swam up and close to the surface of the water. Dessy noticed him, she clapped her hands with the happiness that suddenly overwhelmed her. He finally sees his beloved merman again. She held her hand under the water, and there was no end to her elation.

Dessy didn't see or know that it wasn't her beloved Merman Fasel, but that it was her fiancé Gianni. He took her hand for a short time and suddenly let go, and she was completely delighted by his touch and gesture. As the merman Gianni swam close to the surface of the water, she noticed his blue tail as well. This again truly delighted her. Dessy then abruptly put her hand to her mouth as if in some sincere and genuine disbelief.

- Oh, that's completely impossible! – she said what she really meant in those seconds. Dessy leaned over the water to get a better look at him, but now she couldn't see anything again.

Her beautiful, young face was a source of happiness. Merman Gianni was still swimming calmly, and she watched his reflection in the water without saying a word and with sincere delight . And then she suddenly got serious and was thoughtful.

Where's the orange tail with the orange tail?

That day, they had to sort out some details in the barn. There were: the boss Demetrisio, Dessy and some workers. They were arranging the interior of the barn. It was in the part of the barn where Wicky and the foal Jeanne were. Spidey the blue spider just watched calmly, hidden in the highest corner of the barn, in the fervent hope that he would not be touched again by something as horrifying as that cobweb-sweeping broom. He just calmly watched as all his effort and cobwebs slowly disappeared under their brooms, and that meant that he would now have to work even harder to make new cobwebs.

For a few moments, Demetrisio looked at his daughter, who was diligently helping him in this business.

- Have you finally written to your fiancé Gianni in Rome? - her father asked her. He watched the next few moments.

- I'm going to write to him today - Dessy lied quickly.

He looked at her again, as if he didn't believe a word he said.

- When today?

- Later - she said vaguely.

- You said that some time ago. I think it would be okay for you to answer him – he suggested quickly, and then went a little further to another part of the stable where he devoted himself to the work of grooming horses. Dessy looked at him for a few moments, and then calmly walked all the way to Wicky's horse and hugged him. She smiled.

-Imagine Wicky, there are two mermans there. Isn't that nice? – she stroked the horse Wicky's mane and head, and then calmly went out of there.

Finally seeing that the whole road was now clean and that no one would cover him with a cleaning broom or something even worse than that, Spidey the spider felt that his five minutes of fear had passed. He then calmly descended a little lower all the way to the horse Wicky.

- Did you hear that, Wicky? - said Spidey the spider , looking and thoughtful. - There's two mermans in there.

Jeanne smiled.

- Of course. Bird Tropp has already told us that Gianni came here last night from that Rome and threw a gold coin into the fountain. It's already a marman and I'm dying of curiosity to find out what's going on under the water... – said the foal Jeanna, because it was really big news for all of them there – Dessy's rejected fiancé was now just a merman in Demetrisi's fountain. What a spectacular show, but only for a select audience.

- Then I should go to the Fountain of Desires and find out the details of those chattering frogs.

- That's right, Spidey!- confirmed Wicky the horse.

It seemed like a wonderful proposition – to throw themselves into a new scouting expedition and find out all the details of what they had so beautifully designed.

And, of course, that a little later the blue spider Spidey decided to leave his favorite corner for a short time, which Dessy had just cleaned so nicely with that broom, that the poor guy had to make a nice little cobweb beforehand so that he wouldn't feel simply ruined by the cleanliness. So now, from that small cobweb that he had beautifully made, he decided to go straight to that fountain and find out all the important details about Gianni and what was happening there. And there were certainly interesting novelties.

And when the blue spider Spidey came to the "Fountain of Wishes", there were two frogs on the leaves of the water lilies – Rinnie the toad and Mila the frog, calmly collecting impressions of everything. They first told him a few details of everything that had happened the night before. And the blue spider Spidey was looking at them nemo.

- So, so! – he nodded his head affirmatively

- Exactly as you heard, Spidey - croaked Mila the Frog.

- Well, then our Fasel went all the way ... – the blue spider Spidey blurted out as if in some kind of disbelief. He sighed deeply, even though he knew that sigh would not help him much.

-Yes. Miklay the fish told us that Fasel has now fallen in love with Dessy or that he is on the right path to falling in love ... – said the Snake himself, not knowing whether to comment on the new situation, or to keep quiet.

- Why didn't you fall in love 7 years ago? – asked the frog Mila with sincere amazement.

- Because then he didn't know that he could lose Dessy's interest! - concluded Rinnie the toad very cleverly. Everyone has now realized that.

- Then she's sure to be very surprised when she realizes that this other merman is actually her fiancé to whom she doesn't even write."

And who doesn't even think about writing anytime soon... – Spidey noted. Indeed, the only letter that Gianni received from the stud farm of the owner Demetrisio, was their letter.

- Maybe she'll fall in love with Gianni now! - said Rinnie the toad, but that was such a sad possibility.

- Maybe! - replied Mila the frog carelessly. - But what will become of Fasel then?"

These two shrugged their shoulders quickly.

- We'll find out that enigma soon! - said Spidey carefully.

That afternoon Dessy stood quietly by the fountain, absorbed in her thoughts about the merman that had touched her hand and which had a beautiful blue tail. Were there any more beautiful mermans like the one she had seen with a beautiful golden tail and kissed? – these were some of the questions that haunted this beautiful young girl, but now she felt much better about it all. Her hand was touched , and it was like a feeling of bliss.

And while Dessy stood beside the fountain and thought of that touch, the Merman Fasel was in the middle of it from where he could see it very well in front of him. Now he had a completely different opinion of her and an idea of all this. He was aware that he had made a mistake in inviting her ex-fiancé to come to the "Fountain of Wishes" and insert a gold coin to become a marman. Some of the steps they took recklessly cannot be corrected now.

He stared at her for a few moments, and then finally decided to approach her. He slowly swam towards the surface of the water. He figured out how Dessy had noticed him. Her face lit up when, finally, after so many days of waiting, she noticed her beloved marman swimming towards her. In one fell swoop, despite the fact that it was day, afternoon and that everything must be teeming with the workers at the stud farm of the owner Demetrisio, Merman Fasel dared and slowly emerged outside.

I've been looking at mute for the past few moments. These were special, romantic moments that happen rarely in life and only with special people. Dessy felt really excited when she saw him in front of her. Now Merman Fasel turned all his attention to her. He gave her a very nice smile.

Dessy stretched out her arms towards him, wanting to touch him, and he immediately swam to her. At that moment, there were no workers or people in the yard of the stud farm of the owner Demetrisi.

- Finally! - smiled Dessy, stretching out her arms towards him. You beautiful merman! – their hands almost touched.

- And you beautiful girl ...

Her hands were in his. Their eyes were fixed on each other, and it was as if the whole world had stopped in those beautiful seconds. All their attention was directed towards each other, and they were both unaware of anything else in this world. It was a moment that Dessy wished could last forever.

However, the wonderful moment of romance that had overwhelmed them had suddenly vanished. Namely, the merman Gianni, who had been closely following the movements of his great rival, now noticed what was happening on the surface of the water. As he was filled with a sincere feeling of a real and cold rivalry to the Fasel merman, now Gianni swam to his rival. And in those moments of intense romance between Dessy and Fasel, he pulls the golden-tailed merman down under the water.

The wonderful moments of romance were gone, and Dessy could only see her beloved merman disappear abruptly under the surface of the water.

- What's going on? - asked Dessy, noticing some stirring under the water.

Merman Gianni was very angry.

- You disgusting golden-tailed monster! I told you that we would fight for it. It seems to me that you have become sympathetic to her? – They are now facing each other as if they were in a real ring, ready for a fight.

- You don't like or appreciate, Dessy - Fasel told him, and that was also true.

- Ha, ha ha ha! I will love and appreciate her even less now that I know that she betrayed me by falling in love with you. I'm going to punish her for that one day, when she marries me," he said, filled with real waves of sincere jealousy and hurt vanity.

All this was patiently and calmly watched by two frogs – Mila the frog and Rinnie the toad. They didn't want to take part in this quarrel or fight, sometimes it's better to be just a silent witness in some things.

- I think now we're going to have to help Fasel earn her love.

Rinnie the toad nodded.

It's a shame that the whole situation has become more complicated.

- Maybe it was supposed to be this way - assumed the frog Mila, aware that it was not her job to stuff herself into love affairs and all kinds of romances in the fountain.

- The Office was still looking at me angrily. They were very angry with each other. And the tension between them that reigned in those moments, could be cut with a sword.

- If I had known that you, Gianni, were so insensitive, we would never have called you ... - Fasel said what he really meant.

Merman Gianni just smiled sweetly and triumphantly.

- There is no point in crying for last year's snow...

Fasel, who now had no patience for the arrogance of the merman Gianni, now looked up again at that dear and beautiful figure of Dessy. But as soon as Gianni noticed that the Merman Fasle was heading, he just pulled him abruptly by the tail again and towards the bottom of the fountain. It was as if he didn't want to allow any contact between his fiancée, Dessy, and this golden-tailed rival.

- Where are you going to the rock, stupid merman? - Gianni shouted, and then Fasel began to push him abruptly and forcefully away from him. Then they began to fight underwater, only gradually reaching the edge of the surface of the water. So Dessy could now see that there were two mermans underwater and that something very strange was going on.

However, then, in a brief moment, when the mermans stepped a little further away from each other, the Snake and the fish Miklay took advantage of that moment, getting in the way of them. Now was not the right time for any skirmish between them, and besides, they were not used to fights and such powerful blows.

- Hey, hey is! Society! Stop! – said the Serpent.

-Yes I do. The snake is right. Stop! – replied Miklay the fish.

Mila swam excitedly to them.

- Why are you fighting?

- There's no point in fighting, is there?- asked Rinnie, the toad very promptly and cleverly. It's always better to negotiate than to kill each other. Meanwhile, an angry Merman Gianni stared menacingly at Fasel.

- You're an ordinary, shabby marman and nothing significant in this world, you know!

- And you're an insensitive man who thinks of marrying Dessy just for the sake of money and position in society ... - said Merman Fasel angrily. He glanced briefly at the surface of the water, Dessy was still standing there.

- Now I'm wondering – should I marry her at all? Because if she almost left me because of a stupid merman from "The Fountain of Desires", what will she do when we are married? – Merman Gianni asked himself, but loud enough so that everyone could hear him.

- She'll run to you because you don't have any feelings for her, Gianni - Merman Fasel told him, aware that Dessy must be facing a cruel and empty fate with this Gianni.

- That's not your problem, Fasel!

- You're right – it's not! That may be the problem of all of us now. So it would be best if the real fight started tomorrow, and the one who wins will have the right to go up during the night and take Dessy's love.

- That might be fair! - said Merman Fasel.

Gianni pointed his index finger at him. I could see how angry he was, and how he could barely contain himself from attacking him again.

- Until tomorrow, Fasel! Trust me, tomorrow you won't be back.

He then swam quickly on towards the underwater caves, and they all looked after him in concern and bewilderment, and then they all looked up at Dessy.

12.

The night was a bit cloudy, and the wind was blowing, which seemed to indicate that a little rain was going to fall. The whole estate of the landlord Demetrius fell asleep , and the light in Dessy's room was turned off, indicating that the girl was sleeping peacefully.

It was the perfect time for a conversation between Spidey the blue spider and Fasel the merman, who swam to the surface of the water and held on to the concrete fence with his hands. Spidey the blue spider stood beside him and listened to everything that had happened underwater that afternoon. Merman Fasel told him about the fight that had taken place between the two and the fact that a decisive match between them was necessary.

- Tomorrow is the decisive day, isn't it? - asked Spidey the blue spider.

Merman Fasel thought of all this, convinced that he might not be able to fully sleep that night because of the tense anticipation. He nodded.

- Yes, it's that big day ... – said Merman Fasel carefully. – And I don't like it at all!

- Come on, Fasel, what's to be done, it's not difficult! - said Spidey the blue spider, a little puzzled at all, "that this fight is going to happen.

- It will be a big underwater fight ... I'm sure all the fish will come to watch the fight between the two mermans ... – said the merman Fasel, who didn't feel like doing such activities now.

- It's a shame I won't be able to see it, but I'll be around just in case! - said Spidey the blue spider. Now it would be so good if he were an amphibian or an octopus, that he could witness something so unusual for this horse farm – and that is the battle of two mermans for Dessy's affection.

- And that's some consolation for me.

A short time later, among those dark heavy clouds, the moon appeared in the sky, illuminating the fountain and the figure of Phasel. His face was very thoughtful.

The next day, everything was normal. Only in the early hours of the morning it was raining. So now the soil and grass were damp, and on some depressions small small puddles were created. Dessy, in her usual clothes and red boots, headed for the fountain. As it was a little colder now, she wrapped herself in a nice coat according to the latest fashion. The coat was the color of cyclamen.

Meanwhile, her father, Demetricio, who was sitting at his desk in the office, would occasionally look out the window at the fountain and Desy. There was something of a strange conceit and restlessness in him to which he could not determine the reason and the cause.

Dessy stood next to the fountain. Little did she know that at those moments, a message was slowly being spread down there among the fish and the aquatic world that there would be a great skirmish between the merman Gianni and the merman Fasel. It was news that was transmitted at a very dizzying speed. Everyone knew that there were now two mermans in the fountain and that they were both great rivals who were now fighting for the affection of that girl Dessy. As usual, Dessy's presence didn't mean much to the fish, because they never swam very close to the surface of the water, so they didn't even pay attention to what was happening up there. Now they would occasionally look at the surface of the water and Dessy, who was standing there persistently.

Dessy noticed the color of some of the fish swimming there and smiled happily.

- What an interesting color in the water! – she said quietly.

Some time later, when all the fish from the fountain and all the other interesting aquatic animals that had lived there for a long time had gathered, there was an empty space in the middle of the fountain. And Merman Gianni and Merman Fasel stood opposite each other and gave each other alternate angry glances.

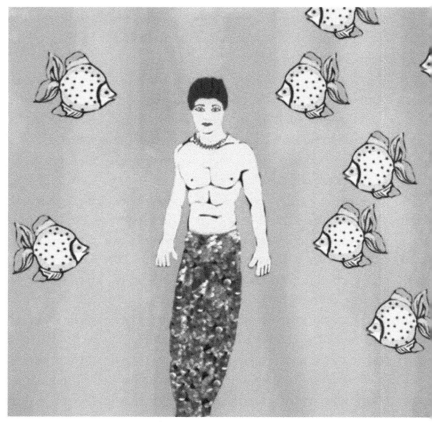

For a moment, Gianni looked as if he was a little out of his mind.

- It's time for me to finally kill you.

Fasel was aware of his intolerance as well as the prominent note of derision that emanated from his rival.

- Try Gianni, just try!

At that moment, between two fierce rivals, Miklay fish stopped. He looked at one of them, then at the other. It's as if it's time for this brutal fight to finally end and for everything to return to normal activities in the fountain. And so, for the past few weeks, they haven't had the wonderful level of water harmony that Dessy's presence has been disturbed at all.

Fish Miklay sighed deeply, and then he made a loud whistle.

- So, let's get started! The fight can begin!

And the two men then approached each other, angrily measuring each other. Merman Gianni shook his head.

- This beautiful victory now you will not take away from me Fasel!

Fasel nodded his head. He's trying to get rid of this disgusting Dessy fiancé.

- You've got to win, Gianni.

And the fight between them began. At first, they hit each other, and then they got into a real fight. The mermans pushed each other away, pushed each other to the ground, crushed each other, and it was a real clash between two strong male forces. All the fish, frogs, and shellfish watched the fight as if in some kind of suspense, and partly in fear and anticipation. It was also the first time they had attended such a match in that fountain, and it was all because of the affection of the girl standing upstairs.

Not far from the fountain, as if in some first uncertainty, stood the spider Spidey. And he was overwhelmed by dark forebodings and strange thoughts about what was to come. The two curious, voracious storks – Tropp and Mexy – flew to him quite calmly.

- Hey, Spidey, what's going on down there? - asked Tropp the stork, who knew about the skirmish that was coming, but as it was a feathered animal with wings and beak, it was not very suitable for swimming underwater.

- Yes, Spidey - Mexy nods. - You seem very upset.

The blue spider Spidey, who had been really upset, was now just looking at them calmly.

- Now the big fight between Fasel and Gianni is underwater. The one who wins the fight will marry Dessy ... – he explained to them filled with some fan zeal. And he was the one who was going to win this fight.

- Hey Mexy, let's stay here with Spidey and find out who the lucky winner is - said Tropp the stork, staring at the Mexy stork, who didn't mind this extraordinary proposal of waiting for the official results of that fight. Even the boss Demetrisio occasionally looked out the window towards the fountain, and noticed is how the storks have now landed very close.

- Yes, come on! We'll stay here!

Down in the water, the battle was still going on. And it seemed impossible to predict who would be the winner in this fight. Everyone was rooting for Merman Fasel. You could see how both of them were straining with all their might to take down their opponent. One moment it would seem that the merman Gianni was winning, the moment Fasel would take over the fight. It seemed that the fight would never end.

The mermans had a very thick layer of skin, so the blows could never be seen in them.

- I've never witnessed a fight like this before!" said the Snake, who seemed to be in a state of tense anticipation.

The fish, Miklay, who had been the referee of this fight, was now just nodding his head calmly.

- Me neither!

Little by little, Mila the Frog would put her hands over her eyes so as not to see these horrible scenes in battle. All this made her really scared.

- Which of the two do you think will win? – she sighed deeply. She watched the fight again, she put her hands over her eyes again.

- I'm rooting for Fasel! – said Miklay the fish.

- I don't think Fasel deserves to win now - said Rinnie the toad. The frog Mila looked at her with a question mark in her eyes. Rinnie the toad just nodded.

- That's right, my dear! After all, he was the one who first wanted to free himself from Dessy. And if it wasn't for his insistence on a tolerable level of water harmony, I don't think Merman Gianni would be here now, we wouldn't be watching this fight; I mean the fight and all in all... – she sighed deeply. - To make a long story short, let's cheer better..

-You're right! Let's cheer! – confirmed Mila the frog quickly.

The fight between the two angry mermans was still very much going on. They hit each other with their hands, fists, they would hit each other with all their strength and with their hands so that for a short time one of the mermans would hit the ground. But he would quickly get up and get back into this fight.

Then, quite unexpectedly, they both came very close to the surface of the water.Dessy saw a strange commotion downstairs. She thought she saw two tails – one golden and one tricise-blue. She was in a hurry into the water.

- What are those two mermans doing downstairs? - Then they disappeared from her sight. The fight took place again near the bottom. And because Dessy was very interested in this exciting, unusual spectacle, she suddenly jumps down into the water.

Her jump was noticed by the boss Demetrisio, who was in the office at the time. He was standing near the window and saw her jump. I was extremely shocked by that gesture. He felt a terrible fear. Without a moment' s notice, he quickly ran out. He knew that Dessy couldn't swim regularly. What was going on with that girl? Is she completely distraught?

- Dessy! Dessy! What are you doing? – He went down the stairs very quickly. It must be admitted that boss Demetrisio as a parent was extremely panicked, he rushed out.

At the time, Dessy was under water. For a few moments, she stared at the exquisite colorfulness and colorfulness around her. For the first time in her life, Dessy saw beautiful fish and noticed two mermans fighting not far from her.

She stared at them, completely shocked by the horrible scene of the fight. She was even more shocked when she saw that one of them was her fiancé, Gianni from Rome. She couldn't help herself from the shock that overwhelmed her. Gianni as a merman? Is her fiancé Gianni Merman with that blue ponytail? It was a question that was completely shocking.

Meanwhile, two storks, Tropp and Mexy, and Spidey , a blue spider, noticed when Dessy jumped into the water, and a minute later, Boss Demetrisio rushed out as if the three devils were hot on his heels.

Stork Trop was amazed and upset, he just glanced quickly towards Spidey.

- Spidey, this doesn't look good to me!
- Not to me! - replied Mexy.

The blue spider Spidey just shook his head.

- Now that the boss Demetriso discovers that he has two mermans in the "Fountain of Wishes", we all have to make a fuss ... – he could already imagine the outcome of such a discovery.

The white cat, who was only a neighbor's cat after all—and you know that you shouldn't get too involved in neighborly problems—just looked at Spidey.

- And why should I bother too? I'm not from here!

Everyone continued to observe the events surrounding this "Fotnana wish". And with the exception of those press conferences, this was now the top event that Gbazda Demetrisio personally engaged.

Underneath the water, Dessy, who could barely hold her breath now, watched the two angry mermans fight. Fasel was the first to notice her and was completely surprised to see her looking at them in amazement and shock. It was something she could not have dreamed of seeing.

- Dessy! - cried Merman Fasel, and he stopped fighting with Gianni.

Then the merman Gianni turned to her. He was surprised when he saw her. She was really surprised to see him there as a merman.

- Desdemona! - exclaimed Gianni in utter disbelief. He couldn't have imagined anything but that she would jump into the water and see them in action. Where did you get that from?

- Ah! - she sighed. Soon after, she put her hand to her mouth, feeling that only that one, small sigh suddenly made her begin to choke. She tried to swim, but now it seemed that she would stay underwater. Then she was grabbed by the hands of the boss Demetrisio. He took a dip in the water and luckily didn't notice that he had two mermans in the fountain. He grabbed his daughter by the shoulder and elbow and barely managed to pull her out of the water. He threw her over the concrete fence and laid her on the ground.

The fight between the two mermans had completely stopped, everyone was now looking at what had just happened. It was not very often that they saw the boss Demetrisio immerse himself in that fountain. In fact, as far as Rinnie remembered, he almost never dived.

Mila the frog and Rinnie the toad, quickly and extremely curious, swam to the surface. Now they were able to watch the events take place in peace. Boss Demetrisio laid his daughter on the ground, and Dessy lay there for a few moments coughing. The girl struggled to catch her breath. Demetrisio was terrified.

The two storks followed it all closely. Boss Demetrisio frolicking in the fountain. It's a real spectacle this summer.

Tropp leaned over to Spidey the spider and said quietly to him:

- Now we're done!

The blue spider Spidey nodded his head.

- 100%!

Meanwhile, very furious, the boss Demetrisio shook his daughter very hard . If he could, he would have put her in a cannon at that moment and fired at the moon, how angry he was at her terrible attempt to jump into that horrible stinking fountain.

- Are you crazy? You jumped into that terrible water.

Dessy, who had finally caught her breath, was now looking at her father in amazement. Now the rest of her family will find out. It's all over with her and her friends. The girl, however, quickly straightened up and sat down. It was completely wet, but it didn't matter. More important were the anger and severity of the boss Demetrisio. Dessy knew she had to pull herself together quickly. Did dad see that fight under the water? What will happen now?

-No! Dad! I am not!

- Why did you jump into that horrible, old fountain? Now I'm sure I'm going to order my stud farm workers to fill that fountain once and for all! – boss Demetrisio said furiously. That's what he almost really meant now. It's time for Dessy to devote time to piano and reading, rather than standing by that horrible, smelly pond all day.

Dessy was terrified at the time. She shook her head.

- No, father! No! Don't do that, I love that fountain...

Boss Demetrisio was now showing his trait of true inexorability.

- But you jumped down!

Then the maid Merkez ran up to them. She stared at Dessy, who was completely wet, and the boss, Demetrisio, who was yelling at his daughter. Dessy stood up while her father looked at her the whole time.

- My beautiful miss, are you all right? - asked Merkez. As if some of her hunches had come true, Dessy jumped into that water.

- Yes, I am - Dessy confirmed quickly.

The two frogs were still watching them very patiently from their favorite leaves of green water lilies.

- She jumped into the fountain and I saved her - said the boss Demetrisio, who couldn't believe what had just happened.

Meanwhile, the two mermans saw what had just happened and were a little numb under the fact that this successful and strict man, the boss Demtrisio, was now involved in all the happenings in the fotnana.

- Boss Demetrisio is here now - said Merman Gianni, wondering for the first time how Master Demetrisio would react if he looked under the water once more and noticed his daughter's fiancé frolicking around.

- It'll be a good thing he doesn't see us here! - said Merman Fasel, who was horrified by the thought.Underwater caves were now the only peaceful way out. It's the only place where Demtriso can't come unless he's extremely persistent.

- It will be good that it does not bury us with earth, at least until midnight passes today.

Fasel sighed deeply, you could see that he didn't care at all.

Meanwhile, the Tropp family, who had heard what the boss Demetrisio had said, could not help but say.

- If he buries that fountain, then Fasel will be better off finally loving his fleas and becoming an ordinary cat again!

Stork Tropp watched as Dessy slowly rose to her feet. Water dripped from her clothes and dripped on the ground. No one was paying attention to that now.

- I lost my ring ... Accidentally ... that's why I jumped down," Dessy tried to make things up. She also pointed to her own hands.

Demetrisio stared at her hand for a moment. Admittedly, it was as if he didn't quite believe in the transparent story she told. He was still very angry.

- And? - asked the boss Demetrisio.

- I found it, father - she sighed convincingly, pointing to the ring. - That's why there's no point in you jumping into the fountain after me.

Boss Demetrisio, to whom this scene had just been like the worst nightmare of every devoted and good parent, now sighed deeply. It was as if he was thinking for a moment about what to do next, he just cleared his throat angrily . And then, with the utmost determination, he grabbed his impossible daughter's hand and began to drag her with him. Merkez, in a somewhat funny way, ran fast and gagged, followed them.

This time, as a result of all this recent shock, the boss Demetrisio was extremely relentless.

- Now! You're going to your room Dessy! You will stay there as if in solitary confinement, for two days ... And then you're going to go to Sicily with secretary Salicil to my sister's and you're going to stay there until further notice!

This was a real nightmare for Dessy. Everything else, except Sicily! Far from the stud farm, from the fountain, from the merman, from love. She couldn't believe that she was hearing what she was hearing and that her father was ready to send her to that distant island in the Mediterranean Sea. All her beautiful dreams would disappear, everything would become just a faint memory. That day was going to end in the worst possible way.

- Or the father ... No!

Demetrisio was unstoppable.

- Go!

Dessy knew she had to get out of this situation somehow. Sicily was like a big trap for her.

- I don't want to go to Sicily.

They were already inside the house, and he was dragging her down the stairs all the time. They spoke very loudly, so that even those who were outside at that moment could hear them. The two frogs on the leaves of the water lily looked at each other blankly. The battle ended in a way that none of them could have expected. Now the mermans have also slowly surfaced. Now they could only be silent observers. They had heard that Master Demetrisio had decided to send her to Sicily, but now neither of them could come to the surface, go to the house and explain to Master Demetrisio what was going on. Now they were just ordinary mermans with a tail.

Tropp ay was truly surprised by these words.

- To Sicily?

And the toad Rinnie wondered what the Blue Ghost was going to do about the whole situation that had ended – really inglorious for Fasel. Now all that remains is a suitable level of water harmony and nothing more!

- And he'll stay there until further notice - croaked Rinnie the toad.

Demetrisio forced his daughter into her room.

- Yes, Dessy! You're going to stay here! I'm going to order someone to go around you and make sure you don't accidentally sneak out of the room... Where's your key? Ah, here he is ... – he was indeed extremely angry and angry. He immediately saw the key on the table and took it in his hands.

- You're going to stay locked up here until I agree with my secretary about your departure. - And you will be in Sicily until further notice. I don't want to hear a single word anymore because my patience has some limits... And I'm tired of that horrible fountain and the fact that you spend so much free time there – he said what he really meant all those last days.

- But Dad ... – Dessy was trying to understand the complexity of the whole situation that had arisen. She was as utterly discouraged as any other young girl would be in such an unusual situation.

- And you'll be in the room. You can't leave the room. I'm expressly forbidding you to do so. And you, Merkez, will bring her only meals in the morning, at noon and in the evening. You will help her pack all her clothes in her suitcases and get ready for her trip to Sicily. I've been watching you on that fountain for days, but the fact that you jumped inside, that's the highlight! All the time he was saying this, he was shouting so that his face flushed with rage. He threatened her with the raised index finger of his left hand – so that he could be heard by all those outside who were waiting for these sudden developments.

Dessy was still in utter disbelief.

- But dad ... You don't understand! There are not only fish there, but ...

Boss Demetrisio, who was now in over his head about the theme of the "Fountain of Wishes" , just sighed deeply. He angrily interrupted his daughter's presentation, because he already did not have an ounce of patience for any rinses.

- And enough more! I don't want to hear a single word, am I clear? I forbid you to leave this room until further notice... I love you so much and you are everything to me. I don't want to lose you! – That is what he really meant very sincerely. He looked at her again, aware that what he feared most now as a parent was never to lose Dessy.

Dessy thought of Merman Fasel, and of her fiancé Gianni from Rome, who looked so beautiful with that turquoise blue tail. He had never given her such an impression of real attraction before. Now it's all over. All hopes and dreams come to an end that her father has determined.She took a deep breath. Maybe if she tried to explain something to him. But what to explain? And how? He will think that she has gone mad and will never understand her. Ah, how hard it is when you're young and you can't explain your crushes to a parent!

- He wouldn't lose me... Down there are...

He interrupted her angrily again.

- Enough with the story! I'm going to make sure she doesn't do something stupid.

Dessy looked at the maid Merkez, who now really couldn't even help her with a cup of coffee when her father got angry, and that rarely happened, no one ever dared to contradict him. The maid was also very worried about her.

- But Father, I'm not...

The maid Merkez spoke very quietly, as if she were afraid that her boss Demetriso would put her in a suitcase and send her with Dessy to Sicily – and that, of course, was not the way she had hoped for.

- As you say , Mr. Demetrisio!

He was still staring at his daughter.

- I told you, Desdemona, I don't want to hear a single word again. I'm going to Sicily and Sicily. There's nothing going to stop me from changing my mind. Merkez! – he shouted very loudly, and the maid quickly collected herself. She was confused by the whole development of this situation, which promised that Dessy would soon go on a trip. She wore a little bit of her blouse and apron, which she always did when she felt anxious.

- Tell me, Mr. Demetrisio!

Demetrisio looked at the maid, then again at his daughter.

- I'm going out of her room now, she's too high for Dessy to escape through the window! - He closes the door and locks the room with a quick and easy move. Merkez, the maid, stood patiently in the hallway with him. A young girl, Dessy, ran to the door and tried to open it to no avail. The door was locked, all her beautiful dreams began to crumble like a great house of cards. Everything was over now. For ever.

- Dad! Dad! Let me go! I'm not your prisoner! Dad . . . - she shouted, even though she knew that her father was now completely relentless and that he would not unlock that door even if someone brought him a mountain of the brightest gold coins for his bank safe.

Boss Demetrisio quickly turns to Merkez. He pointed to the key in his hands, as if the patience he had had during that evening had finally begun to run out.

- There's another duplicate of this key to her room downstairs, and this key will be with me until further notice. - She can't leave the room, and no one is allowed to come in except you, Merkez! Am I clear?

The maid Merkez, who, like a real grandmother, now began to take care of the young girl, who, in addition to being locked up, was also in wet clothes, nodded her head calmly. No one was able to argue with Demetrius.

- I understand you, Mr. Demetrisio.

Demetrisio looked as if he couldn't wait to hear her words.

- Excellent Merkez! I'm going to knock that stupid "Fountain of Wishes" out of her head!

Then the two of them went down the stairs, and Dessy leaned against the door and began to cry.

- No, Dad! This is not an ordinary "Fountain of Wishes ". He will never – never understand me. And I don't want to go to Sicily to live there.

13.

Night descended greatly over Italy and over the great estate of the landlord Demetrisio. A yellow-gold moon shone in the sky, forming the usual night idyll surrounded by a circle of tiny tiny stars that sparkled in the sky. Somewhere in the distance was the roar of nocturnal, feathered owl hunters engaged in their nocturnal activity of hunting mice and small rodents. The wind slowly blew and moved the leaves on the trees at a steady pace. Everything exuded night peace.

On the "Fountain of Wishes", as if by some unknown agreement, there were: Fasel, Spidey the spider and storks Tropp and Mexy who had to agree on something that was important in life for them. It was as if Merman Fasel could not believe what had happened in such a short time, which had completely changed his usual course of life, which he had so serenely led for a long period of time.

- To Sicily?- asked Merman Fasel, trying to figure out where the famous Sicily was actually located.

- Exactly. Tropp told me - said Spidey the spider, who prided himself on his perfectly good knowledge of the important things that were now happening before their eyes.

- We've been eavesdropping! - said Tropp the stork, proud of the fact that he was perfect at it—secrets, the birds of espionage on that chimney from where he could hear perfectly well everything that was going on in Dessy's room, and which led to the girl—whether she wanted it or not—to be sent to that famous Sicily for who knows how long.

We didn't even have to listen. Mr. Demetrisio shouted so much that those in Tungusia must have heard him as well – said the stork Mexy, who really wanted to get some sleep at that time, which was impossible because of the screaming of the boss Demetrisio.

- And where is this Sicily? - swam up to them and the frog Mila, who was worried about everything that was happening. It is as if they have really lost the wonderful bar idyll in which they have enjoyed for so many years.

- Very far away - said the stork Mexy.

- So far that neither you Rinnie nor you Mila, even if you really wanted to, would never be able to bounce back that way - he explained to them slowly.

- It is about 930 kilometers from here to Sicily. And it's not the way for frogs! – said the stork Mexy, remembering that island somewhere far away in the Mediterranean, beautiful plantations and warm weather – which seemed to be a wonderful destination for pensioners, for example. But now she didn't think about where retirees go when they retire.

- But Dessy is going there! – gasped the frog Mila.

- Exactly! And in a day or two! – confirmed the Tropp stork. It was a fact demanded by the landlord Demetrisio, and they, being only ordinary inhabitants of that chimney, could do nothing about it except to pity the beautiful young girl.

- That's what Mr. Demetrisio wanted - said the stork Mexy.

- Merkez packed her bags, and Dessy just cried - Tropp said of the young girl's deplorable condition.

- So she's gone out of here for good? - asked Merman Fasel, fully aware that Dessy would never again be near the Old Fountain, which now seemed like a terrible circumstance. He was completely disappointed with all the developments and was unable to change anything in his life and in hers. She was expecting a trip somewhere very far away, and he just stayed in that pond there ... Now it was the worst idea in his head.

- Exactly! - said Spidey, looking at the Merman Fasel.

- But she has to make up her mind by midnight whether she wants me or Gianni! - said Merman Fasel to the fact which the Blue Ghost had so neatly pointed out, "everything now revolved solely around Dessy's choice.

- She's going to that Sicily to her aunt's house and she's going to stay there for a very, very long time!" sighed Tropp the stork, almost feeling sorry for the young handsome Merman Fasel.

- It looks like Demetrisio is really trying to knock the Fountain of Wishes out of her head - said Mexy the stork.

The fountain may be out of her head, but she's in love with Fasel. The mermaids will never be forgotten... – sighed the spider Spidey , fully aware that if he were in Dessy's place in that room, he would now be crying because of the beautiful merman from the fountain that he will leave here forever ...

- Yes, yes, that's right - Mila the frog quickly confirmed.

- And I agree with that – Rinnie the toad swam up to them, and at first she had been quietly listening to that nightly, secret conversation they were having all the time.

- And if Dessy goes to live in Sicily, which is about 930 km away, I'm just an ordinary, blue spider from the barn, and I'm almost convinced that Dessy will surely wheeze to sadness - observed Spidey the spider, completely convinced of this horrifying fact that stands in front of the young girl's life.

- I agree with that! – said Mila the frog.

- She will never forget everything that happened here - shook the head of Rinnie the toad, who was persistently trying to find an adequate solution to this intricate, love situation with her wonderful, smart, frog brain.

- If only a week earlier you had realized that Dessy was the woman of your aquatic life, we certainly wouldn't have found ourselves in this predicament – if Gianni the merman was there, if Dessy was moving to Sicily, obviously for the long haul! And it's all because of your water harmony! – she said it with a voice full of real accusations, but now there was no point in it.

- You should be a little less harmonious! - sighed Spidey the spider, noticing that he himself sometimes lacked harmony in that dusty corner in that stable, without ever talking about it with the horses.

- Maybe we'd be in a slightly different predicament apart from this! Worse still! - said Rinnie.

- It doesn't matter what kind of crunch awaits us now; some crunch would surely be there ... – sighed Merman Fasel, who felt really terrible about everything that was happening now.

- We need to find a solution quickly! – remarked Spidey the spider and looked at the storks as if he hoped that they had a solution, after all, they are real world travelers, they must have noticed something that would help them in everything. The spider sighed deeply again and looked at the moon above them. It's midnight today, isn't it? He asked, perfectly aware that they didn't have much time at all.

- Yes - confirmed Merman Fasel.

- And why should we care here whether it's midnight or not? - asked the frog Mila, a little confused, and stared at the beautiful merman next to her.

- Because according to the water, magical law, we should obey what the Water Spirit said – rules for up to three days. And since we've cooked up this issue ourselves and invited Gianni from Rome; then I think it would be okay to be completely and fair and hear what Dessy thinks. And exactly at midnight! – he sighed deeply, wishing that they would have another day or two to come up with something smart and cultural.

- Yes, but she's locked in her room now! - Rinnie the toad noticed a fact that made everything difficult for them.

- Well, that's not much of a problem! – sighed Spidey the spider , who finally remembered something that would be helpful to them.

Now everyone else was looking at him in complete surprise.

- How is it not? – asked the frog Mila and looked towards the windows of Dessy's room. But now it seemed to her in her frog eyes like a huge path that she could never embark on with her idyllic jumping.

- Well, there I am – an ordinary spider. I have spider threads. I can steal the key to her room and she can sneak out around midnight. So we will all finally know Dessy's final decision... – he said it completely elated, as if he had discovered some latest law in physics or mathematics. Now they all looked at him in some strange way, as if a heavy burden had fallen from their hearts.

- Yes! – smiled Merman Fasel , aware that finally a nice little solution was in front of them. – Spider threads! We have forgotten that, it is a wonderful means of stealing.

- But then, comrades, it doesn't make so much sense to think ... Spidey needs to write a letter now... – said Rinnie the toad, aware that time was ticking for them. Midnight is about to arrive, and they are still talking about everything here in that fountain.

- Do I write a letter? Again? - Spidey the spider was completely surprised by this suggestion, so he just stared at the old toad, although he didn't comment on anything further because it was the smartest after all.

- And you inform Dessy that you're going to steal a key that must be somewhere in Demetriios' office, and then Tropp or Mexy will take you to Dessy's room, so that she can finally get out of there to the Fountain of Wishes. As soon as she decides who she's in love with and wants to live the rest of her life with – and her, And it will be easier for us too! – said the toad Rinnie, the final solution to the whole complicated situation that had been so burdensome to them.

- If Demetrisio knew about this, I'm sure he would strangle us all!" said Merman Fasel, remembering Demetrisio's boss when he used to be angry and that it was not, of course, a pleasant and attractive situation that he would like to see again.

- Enough with the story! - sighed Rinnie the toad, glancing quickly at the storks, and then at the windows of Dessy's room. - Mexy! Fast! Take Spidey to Demetrisio's office, where he has to steal a piece of paper and a pen.

Everyone was now ready for real action to help the girl in love. Spidey the spider was now the real star of the evening again. So a small blue spider sat on the back of the stork Tropp. Everyone was watching the Tropp Stork take off. Spidey the spider had to hold on to her warm white wings, and the stork hurriedly and calmly carried him to the window of Boss Demetrisi's office.

Unfortunately, there was a light in his office, which indicated that the bastard Demetrisio was still there. He sat quietly at his desk, reviewing some very important documents that were of utmost importance to him in his business life. He was writing something in one of the documents, when at one point he heard a strange commotion in the window. Intrigued by the strange noise, he approached the window, just as the stork Tropp had successfully hidden herself under the window, so that he could not notice her. The whole gang that was in the Old Fountain saw it, so they all took their breath away from real fear when they saw that the boss Demetrisio was in that office. That meant that they would now have to get to the key very carefully.

- He's almost seen us! - said Spidey the spider quietly, to whom that boss Demetrisio had never seemed so terrible as he had that night.

'The last thing Mr. Demetrisio would want to see here is a rolled-up stork and a blue spider from the barn!' said Tropp the stork, who, out of a very important precaution, slowly looked into the office to see what was going on so important. Boss Demetrisio sat at his desk again and, amused with his business records, paid no more attention to them.

Spidey also looked inside, not at all fascinated by the scene in front of him. It would, of course, be very, very much easier if the boss Demetrisio wasn't in that room ... Life was really complicated sometimes, wasn't it?

- When does he go to sleep? We can't be here for long, time is running out. If it's 10 o'clock in the evening, it means it's 2 o'clock in the morning. Uh! We're really in a bind – noticed the spider Spidey as if it was burning under our feet.

- Look at it this way, Spidey, this is happening now and never again! - said Stork Tropp, who almost seemed to enjoy these wonderful moments of the classic theft they were about to embark on.

The group at the "Fountain of Wishes" watched with a lump in their throats as the stork Tropp persistently flew around that window like some little squirrel. Everyone was expecting a completely successful end to this undertaking – the theft of that important key.

- What are they doing there? - asked Mexy the stork, who did not understand why the stork Tropp was flying so stupidly in front of that window.

- Maybe the boss Demetriso is in the office now, so they can't get in - Merman Fasel mentioned this very important and important fact that now only slowed down the whole process.

- And is that the white neighbor's cat? - Everyone then looked at the neighbor's white cat walking down the long branch of the tree towards the stork Tropp and the blue spider Spidey. She was really feline curious.

- Fellow, what's going on here? - asked the White Cat extremely curiously, apparently unaware of the time crunch in which they were. She looked in the direction of the office, but there was nothing interesting about it, except that the boss Demetrisio was writing business documents. But this boring, business-like sight has been seen a thousand times by the neighboring White Cat and has never been fascinated.

- We're waiting for him to finish writing the letter - said the stork Tropp, and glanced quickly into the office. Demetrisio was still there.

- Or go to sleep! - said Spidey the Spider, who concluded that he had already done a great deal of good for all of them, and that he deserved a badge of real promotion.

- Then you will wait. He goes to bed around midnight. He is both a copper and a businessman, he sleeps 6-7 hours a day and brings his work home – said the white Cat, who had already seen the boss Demetrius many times who was sitting at that table until the midnight bell on the cathedral was heard. He was truly dedicated to his work in a diligent and dedicated manner.

- Yes, we can see it ourselves! - Spidey the spider sounded desperate when he said that.

- Usually we are not interested in it, but... – began the Tropp stork, who had never been interested in the business activities of the boss Demetrisi.

- We're in a bit of a mess and time is running out. Do you have to be honest or...

- How can I help you? – asked the White Cat really helpfully, in the way that all neighbors should always work quietly. She looked back at the office, then at their utterly worried faces, aware that she too should do something about it. It is not nice to leave the neighbors to suffer.

- We need paper and a pen. Could you come into the office and steal it from him? – said Spidey the spider calmly, aware that he didn't want to go to the office for a major theft, because the boss Demetrisio, if he saw him, would certainly hit him with the first fly he came across. And that was not necessary for him on this evening —to put his life at such risk for the key to Dessy's room.

- He'll be delighted when he sees me - the White Cat remarked ironically.

- And you, White neighbor's cat, make sure he doesn't see you! - said Tropp the stork, who was really desperate by now, because time was running out at a dizzying speed and they had not yet done anything to help Dessy.

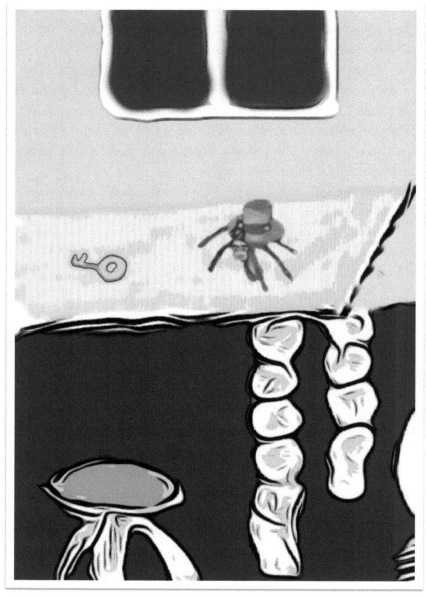

The white cat looked slowly at the office. She noticed a couple of keys standing there. The venture was risky. The last thing Boss

Demetirsju needs, after such a hard day, is the main thief of the evening in the form of the neighbor's White Cat in the office.

- Okay, okay, I'll help you. But if Mr. Demetrisio sees me in his office – I'm done! I'll be a Beijing specialty – sent by express mail! – she said calmly, knowing that this would be the end result of everything – the one on some large Chinese table nicely roasted and salted.

Stork Tropp and Spidey the Spider were now watching very carefully as the White Cat entered the office with a thief's step, the cats were accustomed to sneaking up on their victim, only now the real victim was pen and paper. She walked into the office very slowly, as if she did it about every day. It hung around the feet of Master Demetrisius, but he was now too immersed in the figures he had calculated, which were so important for the banking system. He didn't even notice that the cat had climbed, behind him, onto the chest of drawers from where it had very deftly and quietly pulled out a piece of paper and a pen, and then with that in its mouth it rushed out of the office straight onto the branches of that tree. And then she brought that important and valuable loot to a society that was filled with real anticipation on that "Fountain of Wishes". Roda Tropp flew to them with Spidey the spider on her back. Now everything seemed much easier and better.

Spider Spidey, of course, immediately got to work. He wrote everything that he considered important, followed by the persistent gaze of the society around him, which was envied by everyone because he was so literarily elevated. Now he finished his letter quickly, so he mounted that horse to see his idyllic scribbles.

- So, that's it! Take a good look at the paper. There are a few grammatical errors...

- Come on Spidey, don't get rid of grammar! – reprimanded him Rinnie the toad, who was burning with impatience to finally bring this whole mess to a just and honest end.

- Now she needs to take it to Dessy's room, push it under the door - said Milla the Frog, imagining the complicated process. "She needs to know that Spidey is going to steal the key, bring it to her.

- And why can't I steal that key and take it to her? - asked the neighbouring White Cat, quite thoughtfully.

- Because I think you're too heavy for Stork Tropp to put you on and fly with you," said Rinnie, the toad, who couldn't even imagine the sight of storks and cats flying over the office window.

The young girl Dessy was in her room. She was very sad that she would never have the opportunity to see her beautiful merman again. She was very depressed because she knew that Sicily was very far away, that now she would not be able to eagerly await him because he would stay here forever. Everything conspired against her beautiful, beautiful love, and she could do nothing about it.

Now she just sat sadly on the bed, or rather, she gathered her legs under her and hugged one of her favorite, beautiful, decorative pillows. She calmly sang a sad song, aware that the most beautiful part of that summer was over. Soon everything will be different, she will live a boring and serious life with her aunt, and she will only be able to remember the beautiful merman with a golden tail and probably never forget it.

Now she could conjure up his beautiful face, his fair eyes, and his dark slicked-back hair, fully aware that he was the most handsome man she had ever seen. She quickly wiped away again the small tear that had slipped down her cheek. It seemed to her that she had cried a veritable river of tears by now.

And while she was grieving on her bed because of the hopeless situation she found herself in, she heard a strange sound under the door. When she looked there, she saw a white piece of paper that had apparently been shoved under the door.

She jumped up from the curled up position in which she had been sitting for some time and took the paper in her hands. She read a letter written to her by someone who obviously didn't know grammar regularly, but it was clear to her that someone would bring the key to unlock her room so that she could go down to the Blue Fountain and make a decision about who she wanted to continue her life with - Merman Fasel or fiancé Gianni.

Stork Tropp flew towards Dessy's room. On her back was a spider named Spidey, who also had to hold the overweight key that the boss Demetrisio had just stolen from the office calmly and serenely. He was proud of his successful and successful work.

- Now if we lose this key somewhere, the whole thing will fail ... – said the spider Spidey his very important observation.

- Then stick that key to yourself - said Tropp the stork. Dessy's window was in front of them. They saw a young girl holding the letter in her hands.

- Should I stick the key? – protested the spider Spidey. - Well, this is not a fly or a fly ...

They slowly flew to the window of Dessy's room. Just a few more minutes and everything will finally be resolved. Spidey the spider was now on the window pane, and then he got his threads all the way to the ceiling from where he very slowly lowered the key with one of his threads flat on the surface of the table.

- ...At midnight there is magic... you have to come to the Fountain of Wishes and decide whether you want Gianni or Fasel... and the Water Spirit will then take care of everything – Dessy re-read what was scribbled on that paper. Just as she was putting the paper away from her, she noticed a large blue spider dropping the key on her desk with its threads.

She smiled when she realized that there was a solution to the problem she was facing. The last thing she expected to see was a big blue spider bringing her the key.

- Hey, spider, I already know you, you live in a barn ... – she said to her, completely elated. She stared at him and again in real disbelief at the circumstances in which she found herself. She never dreamed that this old resident from the barn could be of help to her. She quickly took the key in her hands. Time really passed at a dizzying speed. It was already 11:40 a.m. now. She had only twenty minutes left to be at the desired location, and that was the "Fountain of Wishes". She was about to push the key into the door, but then she heard the door to Demetrisio's office open. He slowly, a little drowsy finally decided that it was time to retire to sleep. He really worked a lot that week and the sleep was really necessary for him . Even worse was that today because of Dessy, he experienced real stress, so he couldn't wait to get some sleep. He went downstairs to his bedroom, and she waited impatiently in her room all the time to keep the situation clear.

Finally, at 11:45 a.m., when Dessy was sure her father was in his room, she unlocked the door, elated by the newfound freedom she had managed to gain under extremely strange circumstances.

Very slowly she crept down the hallway. On tiptoe, she slowly climbed down the stairs, hoping that her father wouldn't hear anyone moving down the hallway. And then down the hall, she headed for the door.

- My decision seems to be decisive - Dessy said to herself very quietly. She clutched the key in her hands, not believing that she had a real chance of keeping Merman Fasel for herself forever. She didn't know what tomorrow would bring. But one thing was certain – she would not go to Sicily to visit her aunt.

Meanwhile, Tropp the Stork and Spidey the Spider were showing the impatient company at the fountain the success of this complex endeavor. Now, however, it was really all up to Dessy's decision.

- What are they waving up there now? - asked Rinnie in confusion, staring at the two of them at the window of Dessy's room.

- I think they succeeded in their intention - smiled Merman Fasel kom as if the heavy burden had finally fallen from his heart. Nevertheless, time was still running out inexorably.

- Excellent, that means then Dessy ... – Rinnie the toad began.

- Surely on the way here - finished the neighboring White Cat instead of her.

- Excellent – said Merman Fasel and sighed at that. The most important thing is that they now hear Dessy's final decision.

Merman Gianni finally surfaced, staring at a company that had been chatting here for a long time.

- What's going on? - asked Gianni, looking first at the company at the fountain and then at the lights in Dessy's room.

- We think Tropp and Spidey managed to free Dessy - replied Merman Fasel, who was now really angry with himself for ever daring to invite this horrible young man into his harmonious, bar-like world.

- What do you mean, they freed Dessy? - asked the merman Gianni in confusion and stared at him.

- Well, they stole Mr. Demetriso's key ... - Rinnie began to explain to him very patiently - I think Dessy is finally on her way here ...

- Now we'll find out her final decision ... – said the frog Mila, and closed her eyes for a moment. She really hoped that the young girl would choose none other than – Merman Fasel.

- Yes, Fasel! - said Merman to Gianni confidently, aware that these were the moments of true and ultimate truth. You could have been too involved in her life. I'm currently her fiancé, and right now I'm what she absolutely adores – merman

Merman Fasel turned a quick and contemptuous glance at his rival.

-Yes! But you don't love her!

- Fasel, take it off! – Merman Gianni swam confidently for a quick lap in the fountain. – Let the people live, okay? Go back to the depths of this subterranean lake and be silent – he stood in front of it and smiled victoriously. Now all odds are that he has Dessy all to himself.

Mexy looked towards the exit door, from where Dessy was sneaking out with quite light steps.

- Just be careful - said Milla the frog in a worried tone, staring at the window of Mr. Demetrisio's bedroom , where the light was still burning persistently. "As far as I can see, the light in Mr. Demetrisio's room is still on..." If there's any fuss here at the Fountain of Wishes, I think we have a good chance of being reminded of it, and then...

- We should wait for him to go to sleep - Merman Fasel nodded. He, too, was looking at the window, and the light now had a completely menacing appearance.

Then the real heroes of this night story flew to them – the stork Tropp and the blue spider Spidey , who could finally breathe a sigh of relief. Everything was done exactly as they originally planned. Now this company at the "Fountain of Desires" was filled with real anticipation.

- I think he's done getting ready for bed - Tropp said, staring at the light.

- Where's Dessy? - asked Spidey the blue spider.

Then everyone looked at the young girl who had come out of the house, saw a small group of late-night parties at the "Fountain of Wishes", and then that the light in her father's room, the boss Demetricio, was still on. She just hid behind a tree, waiting impatiently for the right moment to join the company at the fountain that awaited her final arrival.

- Come on, Father! - she said, staring at the light that was still burning. - Midnight is just around the corner. It's Time to Go to Sleep ... I'm really getting impatient – she then looked towards the "Fountain of Wishes" where she could receive her fiancé Gianni and the beautiful Merman Fasel swimming in the water. The sight was truly beautiful under the beautiful, golden moonlight, and she could barely take her eyes off the fountain.

- Oh yes! My decision will be final – Dessy said to herself as if she had to remind herself that it was very important what she would finally decide now.

And finally, to the final delight of everyone at the "Fountain of Wishes", including Dessy herself, who was still standing hidden behind a tree, the light in Mr. Demetricio's room finally went out. Now there are only a few seconds left until midnight. Time passed steadily, and everyone was really aware of that.

Dessy breathed a sigh of relief, nodded her head, and finally walked confidently towards the "Fountain of Wishes". Everyone was watching her coming. But then the midnight bell in the great cathedral was heard in the distance. It was midnight and the right time for the final decision that would change their lives. Never before in those special moments had Dessy felt so important and excited.

Rinnie the toad listened to the sound of church bells in the distance and glanced quickly at the golden moon that shone high up in the sky.

- Now the Water Spirit will come! Guys, we better get out of there – she said to the little frog Milla, and then the two of them hid under the water. None of them wanted to hold a grudge against the sleeping Blue Ghost for rarely waking up, but he seemed very dangerous and menacing in their frog eyes. Spidey and the two storks were now watching from a distance. They didn't want to be seen by the Blue Ghost either. It was as if they were afraid that they would turn them into something completely sixteenth.

- And why do we have to get out of the way, Tropp? - the Spidey the spider turned to Tropp the stork and blinked a couple of times like a real little innocent.

- Because this magic about the mermans is not about you at all, but about them.

While he was saying this, blue smoke appeared from the bottom in the "Fountain of Wishes", which in a regular way started its way towards the surface of the water. Everyone looked on in amazement when the Blue Spirit appeared outside the surface of the water, and now he stood so big and blue above them. He yawned twice, because they woke him up again, and waking up so often had already begun to really hurt him. It must be said that the Blue Spirit was really surprised when all three of them saw them.

- Ho-ho! – he said in his cheerful tone, looking at the two mermans and the girl who stood frightened to the side. Dessy was frightened by the blue appearance of the ghost, which looked like a monster in her eyes. She didn't even know that such a being lived in her phonata. It's been three days, hasn't it?

- That's right, three days - said Hey Merman Gianni in his triumphant manner.

The old Blue Ghost then stared at the young girl who was standing there, her heart beating hard with fear.

- And who are we seeing here?

- This is her, Dessy ... - he began to explain to Gianna, staring at his beautiful fiancée.

- Dessy? - asked the Blue Ghost, fixing his eyes on her.

- My faithful Dessy, because of whom I became a merman, and because of whom I fought with the Merman Fasel - explained the Merman to Gianni in short lines.

- Yes, yes ... – it could be noticed that the Blue Ghost was strangely thoughtful about the whole situation in which both the mermans and the beautiful girl from the stud farm were.

- Hail! Normally I sleep peacefully, but I heard some noise today ... Drum beats! The Blue Ghost said, as if he wanted to complain to someone.

- They weren't bugs - said Merman Gasel, staring at the Blue Ghost.

- That's what we were fighting ... – explained the merman Gianni, almost completely proud of the fact that he had once managed to fight with someone in a real green pond as a marman.

- Yes, yes, it's all clear to me - replied the Blue Spirit, who had been lured back by his dream. It's as if he's been waiting to end up with this company here and he's in the midst of a beautiful decade-long wishful dream.

- Fights without a winner and no end – said quietly Merman Gianni, who seemed to be blaming himself for not being able to properly stand out as the final winner in this fight.

- But someone should put an end to all this, and that's you! - The blue ghost smiled happily and in the manner of a true water gentleman looked at the beautiful girl who was still standing there patiently.

- That's right, Dessy. Tell him that we are engaged and that you can't wait to marry me – her fiancé Gianni looked at her, aware that it was finally time for her to turn only to him and forget about this beautiful merman with a golden tail from his fountain.

- Is it true? - The blue ghost looked at the young girl with a dose of real patience.

- Well... – Dessy began slowly. She glanced quickly at Merman Fasel, who was looking with real anticipation, and at Merman Gianni, who seemed so confident. And then she turned her eyes to the Blue Ghost again. Yes, that was the final moment!

- Still, Dessy, remember how many letters I wrote to you while that stupid Merman Fasel left you waiting and waiting for you...- He even invited me to come here and become a meramn so that you would fall in love with me... And look at him! – Merman Gianni, like a real plaintiff, pointed the index finger of his right hand right at Merman Fasel. He knew that Dessy was his fiancée, and he didn't want her to be near that crappy golden-tailed merman anymore.

- That was before - Merman Fasel seemed to have felt the weight of his unreasonable action when he invited this disgusting Gianni to the "Fountain of Desires." It was something he did in a real way. He hoped that Dessy would understand him...

- When before? And how much sooner? Please, water soul, make me a man again so that I can marry my fiancée nicely – said Merman Gianni confidently, as if he could not wait to become an ordinary man again, get rid of that beautiful tail and water, and finally return to his hometown. He had so many responsibilities ahead of him. The time of squabbling and tinkering with the tail is finally over. He wondered if he should finally breathe a sigh of relief.

The blue ghost was brooding over the whole situation. He turned his gaze to Merman Fasel, who was now really uncomfortable.

- Merman Fasel, do you have something you would like to say or do?

- Dessy, he doesn't love you! - said Merman Fasel what he thought was the real truth.

- Beans. It's funny that you're saying that - laughed Merman Gianni, who once again got the real urge to fight with this horrible golden-tailed merman. Dessy's affection was worth fighting.

- He marries you only for position and money and social success - continued Merman Fasel to say what he thought was true. That girl needs to open her eyes in time. It would be foolish for her to marry the merman Gianni, then find out the real truth, and live her whole life with an empty and utterly sad life.

- It's not exactly that... yes I do... But it's not possible, did Merman Fasel fall in love with Dessy? It's too late for you and your emotions. You are an ordinary aquatic reptile, you could not give her anything special and life. You don't have any money – said Merman Gianni, looking at him with a defiant look. Indeed, what girl would ever agree to marry an ordinary poor reptile living in a fountain? Not even Demetrisio would have allowed it. It would be an impossible love. He values success and power, not love and a golden tail.

- Money? - the Blue Ghost interjected, looking at one merman and the other. - Ah, that's the least of the problems at the moment. So, pretty girl, tell me what you've decided.

Stork Tropp listened attentively to all this from a convenient distance. You could see that he was really impatient about it all.

- I'm just waiting to hear the decision! - he whispered quietly to Spidey the spider, who was standing next to him the whole time with the same anticipation inside.

- Yes, I admit that the situation at the fountain is very delicate - remarked the blue spider Spidey, who was rooting for Merman Fasel, although now everything was in favor of Dessy's fiancé.

Dessy looked at the merman one at a time. She wished she could remember forever those beautiful moments on the 'Fountain of Wishes" that she was sure would never happen again in her lifetime.

- If I choose you Gianni ... I'm going to marry you, I'm going to live in Rome, I'm going to be part of the best Roman social circles... – she said it slowly. She could almost imagine it all and conjure it up in her head. Her father's journey was still ahead of her.

Merman Gianni nodded his head calmly.

-That's right.

Dessy went on with her story, fully aware that even if Gianni would provide her with everything her heart desired, he would not be able to provide her with happiness . But what good is the whole life today if we are not happy?

- But ... but ... – almost as if someone had hit him, this was what that self-confident Merman Gianni looked like now, who was now staring at his fiancée in disbelief. He wondered if he had heard her words correctly.

- And Fasel .... At first you didn't like me and now I turned the tables ... I don't know what it would bring me in life, but – she paused for a moment or two, staring at her beloved merman. The future is an enigma, isn't it?

Dessy looked at one of them, then at the other. The blue ghost was in a great mood even now, although it was already time for him to return to his desired sleep.

- Oh-ho! So, have we made a decision? – Blue Spirit asked her.

The blue spider Spidey quickly turns towards the stork Tropp.

- Well, maybe the water spirit will turn her into a mermaid in that case.

- A mermaid? So, what's the façade? Lake merman? – asked the stork Tropp, who didn't want anyone to watch him in this unique, unrepeatable, spectacular party at the "Blue Fountain"

The water ghost was still smiling as he looked at the girl.

- Well, girl, we don't have all night to spare!" he raised his hand quickly and looked at his eternal wristwatch. "I've been here for a few minutes now, and I'd like to go back to my nap." Getting up at night is already irritating.

He doesn't get up that often. Every 200 years – the spider Spidey noticed what was a clear and obvious fact. How nice it is to have a perpetual job, just to sleep, to wake up every hundred years for three minutes because of someone's special wish.

Dessy was still looking at both of them.

- What's smart to choose? Gianni – a polite and familiar, but happy future? Or you, Fasel – suddenly a love requited, but uncertain future days? – she said quietly, with a pensive face.

- So? Or-or? - yawned the Blue Ghost, letting her know that he was really too awake now.

Dessy narrowed her eyes for a moment.

- I decided ...

- Please, Dessy! - came the pleading tone of the merman Gianni, who was really hurt by the fact that she wouldn't be happy with him.

- I'm choosing you, Fasel! - she said and stared at the merman Fasel, who was surprised, as if he hadn't quite hoped until the last second that she would choose him.

It can be said that all the animals were completely joyful. Milla the frog and Rinnie the toad happily began to swim under the water, aware that their final plan had come true and succeeded. And the spider Spidey cheerfully hugged the stork Tropp and kissed him on his beak.

- I know I'm just a spider, but I just have to do this - he said, joyfully aware that this was probably the only moment in his life when he could kiss a stork in complete peace.

- Then it's my moment to carry out the whole spell to the end - said the Blue Ghost, aware that it was time to bring everything to the final end. A young girl had chosen Merman Fasel, and now he had to put everything in order so that their further life would be led by her decision.

- Dessy, if that's what you've decided, then you'll never see me again. The water spirit will work magic that will erase me from your lives, as if I had never been present – Merman Gianni told her in a pleading voice , staring at her in utter disbelief. It wasn't something he wanted to hear. Did he mean so little to her?

- I'm glad the girl Dessy made her decision. You heard her, didn't you? - the Blue Ghost's voice was heard.

- Yes, but...– stammered Merman Gianni. Now his cruel self-confidence is finally gone.

- And you remember our agreement, don't you? - the Blue Spirit reminded him of their agreement until three nights ago. Now it seemed so far past.

Then the Blue Spirit made a real little blue cloud in which he and Gianni could be seen while they were talking at that fountain three nights ago . You could also hear those words: " ... In that case, you will return to the form of a man, but you will not be here... You will already wake up in your room ... you'll forget you ever knew Dessy and Mr. Demetrisio! You'll forget that you've ever been here, that you've seen me, that you've been a marman. You're just going to have complete amnesia!" Then that cloud of remembrance completely disappeared and evaporated before their eyes. The blue ghost stared at the Merman Gianni for the next few moments, and then nodded reluctantly.

Merman Gianni couldn't believe this was happening to him. He's always been a real winner in everything. Now he felt like a perpetual loser.

- I agreed to that bargain! And now, unfortunately, I lost ...

- We have to stick to the agreement, boy - the Blue Spirit reminded him of the rules of every game - it's important to be a fair player.

Then the Blue Spirit performed his new spell to the delight of all the other onlookers. He snapped his fingers, so that the German Gianni appeared above the water in blue smoke, spun around a few times, utterly surprised by what was happening to him now, and then both he and the Blue Ghost completely disappeared from the "Fountain of Wishes"

It can be said that Spidey the spider could not believe what he saw in front of him. A real little water magic that ended to the delight of all onlookers – just as they wanted.

- I think Gianni has left us, isn't that Tropp?

The blue ghost then flew at the speed of true light to Ginny's apartment. They landed in Rome in his room, where Gianni, now with his legs and in his pajamas, found himself in his bed. With just a quick movement of his hand, the blue ghost made all of Dessy's pictures and letters disappear from Gianni's chest of drawers, and therefore from Gianni's memory. Then the Blue Ghost disappeared from Gianni's room the moment the young man woke up in his bed.

Gianni sat there for a few moments. He nodded and glanced at the clock.

- Midnight has passed. I slept really strangely. Crazy... A wacky dream ... – he laughed when he said that, and then turned to the other side, lowered his head pillow and continued to sleep peacefully. He no longer remembered Dessy, and the estate of the landlord Demetrisio.

The blue spirit then returned to the "Fontain of Wishes" at the same speed of light . His work for that evening, and he hoped for that century, had not yet been completed. He paused at one point, and looked at the merman Fasel, who was swimming in the water in confusion, and at Dessy, who was looking at it all with fear mixed with real elation.

- So, so! True love won in this case, and since it's true love, I think I should be completely constructive ...

- Would you turn me into a mermaid? - asked Dessy confusedly, fervently hoping that she would now be by her beloved Merman Fasel forever.

- Of course not! - the Blue Ghost quickly waved his hand. That really didn't even cross his mind. Lately, there have been too many who have been looking to become tailed, aquatic reptiles. He has already become a bit bored of constantly fulfilling the same desires. What is it to people today when they are attracted only by the idea of swimming, water ...

- Your father would never allow me to do that! - he said, calmly, knowing that Master Demetrisio would surely attack him violently if he found out that he had turned his daughter into a mermaid.

- With gold? - asked Merman Fasel in confusion.

- Well, because he has a golden tail - explained the Blue Ghost, looking at Dessy, who was delighted with the idea. If her father understood anything well in this world – it was the value of gold and money.

- This Fasel is going to be a rich man, isn't he? – whispered the blue spider Spidey quietly towards the stork Tropp. That was the last thing everyone expected, though. The blue ghost seemed to be a real water magician.

- I think that's the ideal option - said the Blue Ghost calmly, as if he had seen their entire lives in the distant future. You're a fancy modern girl, and your father is a banker. Gold is the most ideal variant in this case. So – Fasel! – he said it a bit thoughtful, but perfectly aware that it was the best choice for all of them. He snapped his fingers, and then, to the surprise of all onlookers, the Merman Fasel found himself above the water in all its beauty, with a beautiful golden tail.

- It really has a very nice golden tail - remarked the White neighbor cat, who had been following it closely, so that tomorrow she could tell all the chickens she came across in the area.

Merman Fasel was still hovering above the water. He and Dessy smiled at each other, aware that it was true that true feelings and love always win. To everyone's surprise, the Blue Ghost cracked his fingers again and the Merman Fasel disappeared from their sight entirely. Meanwhile, according to the established schedule, the Blue Ghost lifted Dessy off the ground and quickly found himself in her room with her . He put her to bed and made her fall asleep in a second. Then he changed her framed picture instead of her fiancé Gianna, put Fasel's photographs, and instead of Gianni's many letters, they were now Fasel's letters, Fasel's bouquets of flowers with beautiful dedications in golden letters... And the Blue Spirit continued at the same pace of changing their known history. Landlord Demetrisio went to the room, who was sleeping peacefully, unconscious of the real morning on the "Fountain of Wishes". There is a Blue Ghost changed some contracts, pictures, Phasel's letters ... When it seemed to him that he had done everything first-class, only suddenly the boss Demetrisio disappeared from the room, who was still snoring peacefully on his bed.

The company has now gathered again for a "Fountain of Wishes". Everyone was stunned, elated at the same time. This is a truly unforgettable evening of spectacle for all of them. It is a pity that such interesting, magical evenings cannot happen every evening ... But it would be really tiring for that Blue Ghost who so obviously hated it when he was there every two hundred years ...

- Dude, did you see what I saw? – blinked the stork Tropp, who seemed to be unaware of everything that was happening now.

- Yes, the mermans have left the Fountain of Wishes - said Spidey the spider, aware that now neither Gianni nor Fasel would be there anymore. Ah, what a pity! And almost everyone has gotten used to their rivalry and slingshots around .

- But where is Fasel now? – asked the frog Mila, who was sitting on her water lily, confused, aware that none of them now knew where Fasel was now.

- I have no idea - said Rinnie the toad , aware that she would have to inform all the residents at the Fountain of Wishes about this in the coming days. This magical night will now surely be recounted by all possible generations.

- How about we wake up the Water Spirit again and ask him? – asked the spider Spidey, who suddenly didn't have such a terrible thought of waking up that Blue Ghost again. And so they've been waking him up a little bit lately. I'm sure he's already used to it.

- I don't know... – the neighboring White Cat shook her head in confusion.

- I don't think that's a good idea - said Rinnie the toad.

- Maybe it will turn us into frog drumsticks or some other specialty ... You've heard that he feels like sleeping a while ago – remarked the frog Mila, aware that the best thing to do now is to let that Blue Ghost enjoy his dream realm somewhere at the bottom of the lake where he has been living for a long time.

- He doesn't seem to like it when he's around so often... Every 100 or 200 years.

- I'm just waiting for the morning, to see the continuation of these spells - said the blue spider Spidey, who knew that he would tell everyone in the barn these details tomorrow.

- Just so you know I'm waiting for that too – confirmed the neighboring White Cat, aware that now everyone will be eagerly awaiting the morning to see the continuation of this night's strange story with spectacular twists.

- It's only a couple of hours. I don't know, but I'm so impatient to find out that I'm definitely not going to sleep – stammered Spidey the spider who really didn't feel like sleeping at all now.

They talked a little more about the real impressions of the whole night, knowing that these were those moments that none of them would ever be able to forget.

14.

The next morning, it dawned as it does every morning at the Stud Farm, Demetrisio. The sun shone through its orange-pink rays in the east in the very early hours of the morning , which made it clear that the day would be real summer and warm. The sky was clear blue, with no clouds in the sky. In the distance, flocks of wild ducks could be seen, flying somewhere. The two storks slept peacefully upstairs on the chimney, the only one to hear was the singer who croaked neatly every morning and thus woke up all the animals, as well as the people.

The horses slowly came out to the green pastures to graze peacefully, and the birds in the trees began their usual daily ritual of flying, flying from branch to branch and chirping.

Little by little, all that morning noise outside woke up Dessy. She slept peacefully, reclining in pillows and covered with a thin, summery, silk sheet. A persistent whining that had been repeated so often made her open her eyes and stare at the white ceiling above her. It was as if some images from last night's events flew through her mind like a very slow motion movie. And then the young girl straightened up in bed and ran her hand over her forehead.

"Wait," Dessy asked herself confusedly, "was this all just a strange and strange dream?" she got up immediately afterwards and stared at the bed where she was sleeping. She shook her head, with the vague impression that she wasn't the one who had come to her bed last night, she couldn't even remember when she'd changed into her nightgown last night. Really, what happened last night? She looked around in confusion , and then began to change quickly. No doubt, the last thing she remembered, or perhaps it was just some strange summer dream, was that she was on the "Fountain of Wishes", surrounded by animals, a Blue Ghost and two mermans. Merman? She paused, utterly confused, and then sat down on the bed.

The mermaids don't exist. These are mythical creatures. Men who are only partially eared, and have tails instead of legs – logically they didn't even exist. She squeezed her eyes together for a moment, feeling that everything was very blurry and strange. She walked over to the window and looked at the fountain in the courtyard. It was as if she remembered some strange pictures from last night. She then walked over to the mirror, ready to do her morning toilet. She combed her hair, put on her favorite ribbon, put on her own, loved ones, red boots and a skirt on black puffs. And just as she was about to go downstairs and go to the fountain, to make sure that there were no strange mermans with glittering tails there at the moment, she heard a knock on her door.

- Go ahead!—she said quickly as she put on her favorite lip gloss on her lips.

She turned to the newcomer. It was her father, who was in a very good mood early in the morning. Strange, Dessy thought, shouldn't Dad go to the bank to work?

- Where are you Dessy? Ahhh – he said it in an unusually cheerful tone. Boss Demetrisio had never sounded so great as he did that morning. What happened to him? she wondered.

He came closer to her, and waved with some contract that he already held in his hands. He smiled at her and revealed a series of beautiful white teeth.

- Even today, our young Marquis de Goldy will deposit a few tens of kilos of gold here. "Isn't that excellent, Dessy?" he said with a beaming face, as he always did when talking about money or gold. He stared at the contract he had in his hands, at the numbers that were piling up there, and Dessy, utterly confused, only blinked her pretty eyes. She didn't even know what to say to him now.

Stork Tropp,who was genuinely interested in all the further circumstances of the morning in the house, sat quietly on that branch and listened to the conversation.

- Marquis de Goldy? - asked the somewhat sleepy stork in confusion.

Dessy continued to stare at her father as if devastated.

- Marquis... gold? She blinked again, trying to understand who her father was talking about now. After all, he never burst into her room at dawn with any banking and business contracts.

- If you don't, Dessy. Well, all the week we have been talking about the Marquis de Goldie leaving a lot of gold in my bank. And I, if an excellent banker, can say that today a lot of things will lose their value, but not gold ... – said it again in a very proud tone.

- Marquis de Goldy? - she repeated again, and could have sworn that she had never known anyone with that name in her life.

- You can see you've only just gotten up, honey - her father stroked her hair very patiently.

It was only then that Dessy remembered the beautiful golden-tailed merman in her fountain, its light eyes, its dark slicked-back hair, its beautiful shoulders... She shook her head, though she was still confused as to how her father knew about him now. And she still calls him by that name? It was her marquee, not a marquis.

- Beans? Oh yes! Of course, I'm up now, Dad ...

Demetrisio smiled. He looked as if that day was completely magical for him already in the early dawn. He walked towards the door and turned to her once more.

- Okay, okay. Wake up, and come and have breakfast. Fasel had just arrived from Paris—and while he was standing at the door, so serene and delighted at the good bank-shop , he gestured with his hand to the framed picture that stood on her chest of drawers. Only then did she turn her gaze towards the painting. Now, instead of the picture of the other man, whose name she had now suddenly forgotten, there was a picture of her beloved Fasel.

- And I think he looks really nice there - her father added, and then quickly went outside to look at the contracts once more.

Dessy just walked over to the picture that was standing on the table. It was her Fasel. She stared at his face, and couldn't decipher through the clouds of mist in her mind when she had even put the picture in that frame. That image of water must have been standing for a long, long time. Maybe for weeks or months. It looks like she and Fasel have known each other for a long time? Her father is delighted with Fasel. But she couldn't remember any other details except that it was a merman. Or maybe she was just dreaming last night?

-Yes, of course... Fasel and gold! – she stroked the picture as she had caressed the surface of the water in the fountain before, and put the picture back on the chest of drawers.

Stork Tropp almost fell off the branch when he heard all this talk. I was extremely surprised.

- I think the company will be surprised to find out how far Fasel has come! - he said it calmly and then flew towards the barn to tell the whole company in the yard the latest news, which everyone was now eagerly awaiting.

In front of the gate and the entrance to the stud farm, Demetrisio, father and daughter were now standing side by side with great anticipation . Dessy put on her formal dress and favorite shoes as she scrambled from foot to foot, waiting for her fiancé Fasel to arrive. The father spoke of him very cheerfully all the time .

- I don't usually expect anyone in front of the entrance, and you know that, but now it's a special situation.

Dessy looks at him quickly.

- Of course, father!

- And we'll have to arrange everything we need for your wedding in 20 days - said the landlord Demetrisio, as if he had just thought of that spectacular day when his daughter and young Fasel would finally get married, and their assets would merge into one big wealthy unit. It was a day that every banker would look forward to with great excitement.

Dessy was startled. No one mentioned it to her. Twenty days? Wedding?

-Wedding? Yes, of course.

- I've been hearing this for months that Fasel is this, if Fasel is that ... And what wedding dress are you going to wear! – he reminded her very nonchalantly, and for a moment she stared at the ground very confused, because she didn't even know where else to look.

- Yes, of course, for months! – she confirmed after him, although she still didn't remember anything.

Demetrisio breathed a sigh of relief, as if a heavy burden had fallen from his heart.

- But let's get rid of that story now, here it is. Fasel's car – he then gestured with his hand towards a very luxurious car that was speeding towards them. The Marquis Fasel de Goldy had so much money in his bank account that he could always buy the best cars and everything he wanted in the world. The luxury Mercedes sedan was slowly approaching them and it was the latest and most expensive car modzel in Europe.

- It's nice to be the richest gold dealer in Paris, isn't it, Dessy? - Demetrisio said it proudly, with a voice quite happy that his sweetheart now had such a wonderful fiancé.

Finally, the luxury car stopped in front of them.

Young Fasel came out of the car very elegant and well-groomed. He was dressed in the latest fashion, wearing a gold expensive watch on his wrist and beautiful shoes. It was a symbol of true French elegance. When the young man approached them, he first looked at his beautiful Dessy with loving eyes, and then came closer to the boss Demetrisio. The old man smacked him on the shoulder very quietly and nonchalantly.

- It's nice to see you again and to work with you, young Marquis Fasel! -they shook hands.

- It's nice to see you, Mr. Demetrisio - Fasel said with a noticeable French accent in his voice. And then he finally looked up at his beloved Dessy and the two finally fell into each other's arms.

- Yes - thought Dessy, - this was what I had always dreamed of, had long dreamed of. And that's the most important thing" – she thought to herself as she enjoyed that long and beautiful kiss, aware that if there was ever anything important in this world, it was true love.

In twenty days, the two were finally married as befits the Marquis Fasel De Goldy - Fasel and the young Dessy, the daughter of the respectable and wealthy banker boss Demetrisio. It was a wonderful and very eventful wedding where there were many guests and happy guests who were looking forward to the wedding. The wedding was held in the courtyard of that beautiful stud farm with beautiful, white chairs on which the guests sat and beautiful wedding wreaths.

When the newlyweds finally said "I do" to each other and kissed, and journalists neatly recorded it in their notebooks, and photojournalists took pictures of that solemn and significant moment.

The storks sat quietly on the chimney and watched the whole event. And the emotional Tropp just wiped away tears when he saw happiness on the young married couple.

- I'm always saddened by happy endings.

Mexy just looks at him and continues to follow the ceremony at the "Fountain of Wishes".

- You've always been like that.

The next day, all the newspapers carried a picture of their beautiful wedding on the front page with the text "The richest jeweler from Paris and Demetrisio's daughter got married ". People bought these newspapers and read about them with interest and enthusiasm.

And we will end this beautiful story from the stud farm of the owner Demetrisio by revealing to you how they lived forever happily ever after . But in the "Fountain of Wishes" of the boss Demetrisius, marmans were never seen again. At least not at this age.

THE END!

The novel is based on the screenplay of the same name for an animated film for children.

Author: Dianna Diverno
    Novel : Dessy and Mermen
    Translation: A.B
    Novel Writing Date – April 2023 – September 2024

Milton Keynes UK
Ingram Content Group UK Ltd.
UKHW030745221024
449869UK00001B/66